Author Stephanie Barbé Hammer takes us on another wild ride through the world first introduced in Narrow Interior, this time on a train in search of a missing immigration activist. From a boy in a kilt to an octopus in a girl, pull up a meticulously restored antique bench in the observation car to enjoy tall tales, acts of bravery, and young love. As Mack reminds himself, "try to think like a detective, not an asshole."

—Kathleen Alcalá, author of *Spirits of the Ordinary*

Journey to Merveilleux City is a mystery novella about the ways in which people in the 21st century communicate with each other, often creating and often missing meaning. These talk, text, blog, vlog, and write. Some willfully misrepresent or refuse to respond. Some argue with their inner selves, who abuse and shame their outer selves. All the while, Hammer explores how communication reveals who we are to ourselves and to others. *JTMC* is a brilliant piece, building on, but not dependent on, her earlier work. Hammer has created a universe that can be read and reread, a universe that reflects the wildness of our own.

—John Brantingham, author of *My Dead*

Journey to Merveilleux City

Stephanie Barbé Hammer

Picture Show Press

Published by Picture Show Press

Cover Design by James, GoOnWrite.com

ISBN: 979-8-9850690-3-7

First edition 2023

Contents

Introduction: Greetings from May-Bel to her vlog viewers

Hello dear viewers! This is May-Bel the Happy Train Vlogger from Chongqing, China!

Today is the final stage of our Chongqing University trip travelling through the U.S. by train. What a delightful and educational journey. How refreshing to discover that American trains aren't faster or cleaner than at home in China! We felt relaxed! We were not intimidated!

Today, I have the special privilege of travelling by myself from Narrow Interior Town in the eastern part of the U.S. to Merveilleux City in Canada. Voyages Rétro makes a special old-fashioned train. That is the train I will be taking; keep watching for the best sights and sounds from this trip! Then I will meet my class in Merveilleux City for a visit to the Nouvelle Université des Ideés Curieuses. I received special permission to take this train, and I promised to rejoin my class on time!

Here is a map of the train I am taking today. In the front is the engine of course. It is an old engine, but it is fixed to run on diesel and not coal. This makes less smoke, but I like electricity better because of global warming. Next is a baggage car and after that the car for first class and second class. I wanted to buy a second-class ticket so maybe I can meet other students, but the people here say that I am an important Chinese travel vlogger, so I have a first-class ticket for second-class money. Lucky!

At the end of the train is a dining car with very good American food. The last car is called the Observation Car, and that is the place where everyone goes to talk, meet new people and look at the scenery. There is even a little balcony at the very end of the car, enclosed by a wrought iron fence. A person or two can stand on this balcony, in the outside air, and maybe have a cigarette while the train is moving.

I am thankful to have a first-class ticket, but I think I will like the Observation Car. Maybe I can go there and meet students like me?

Just a note, this English language version of my vlog is new. This will be an opportunity for me to practice my English and hopefully reach a wider audience. People from China, just a reminder that you can click on the link in the notes below for the Chinese version of this vlog.

Time to go. Welcome Aboard and thanks for watching!

1

Mackinnon Macdonald Flores is not looking for romance

What the hell was I thinking wearing a kilt in this drafty old New England train station?

My legs are cold. No, actually what's really cold is my ass. The way the wind kicks up here and it's March! Back in San Dimas it's hot already. Well, warm.

My best self, whom I dub Inner Mack—as opposed to my pissed off usual self, whom I just dub me—says:

Relax. You promised your dad you'd take a trip cross-country, and now you have. You promised him you'd check out the historic town of Narrow Interior, and now you have. You'll train up to Merveilleux City Quebec and then you'll go straight to the Bagpipe Band Conference Welcome Kiosk at the Convention Center. You'll find the pipe band members, and then you'll hang out, take part in the workshops and drink some beers.

But I'm cold! I re-explain to him. Why couldn't I spend my vacation in like San Diego or something?

Relax. This is the last Spring Break before you get your Teaching Credential. It's good to do something social.

I'm plenty social!

Relax, take a breath, and get your flipping ticket.

You don't mess with Inner Mack when he tells you to breathe. So I take a San Dimas Serene Awareness™ cleansing breath and I go stand in line on the worn-out looking floor as I await my turn at the worn-out looking counter of this worn-out looking train station in this worn-out looking town, Narrow Interior, Massachusetts. Man, it's weird how everything on the East Coast is so old looking—beat-up, grey. And freezing.

My mom and my sister text me:

> How's it going, Mack? We miss you.

Bullshit. They're just glad I'm not sleeping on the couch at my mom's anymore.

> Meet anyone yet?

That's got to be my mom.

I text back:

> The last time I met someone it did not go well. As you may remember. She got everyone in my graduate film studies program mad at me because she told everyone I was a complete asshole. So I had to change schools and programs and get my teaching credential instead.

> Well Mack, you are an
> asshole some of the time

That's my sister.

YEAH BUT WHO ISN'T? I type.

Inner Mack intervenes:

Breathe and be nice.

I breathe and delete my text.

I spot a couple of other guys in kilts. We wave. "See you on the train!" one guy shouts. He's older—a lot older.

Most of them are older like that. Most are white.

At least this one didn't hesitate before waving like a lot of them do.

A lot of times when the pipe band guys see me, they kind of do a double take and go like ... *hmm* ... *What is he?*

They aren't expecting a combination of incredibly tall Highlander mixed with a surprising dab of Che Guevara.

That's when this lady a couple of people up from me in the longish line starts talking loudly in Spanish. Then she looks back, sees me, and starts gesturing wildly for me to come talk to her.

"Save my place, will you?" I say to the guy in back of me.

Speaking of white guys: the one behind me is a big white dude with a weird t-shirt that looks like an American flag but isn't, and he kind of scowls, but I say, "Gee, thanks man," which is what you have to do when you're a teacher (take charge and proceed).

I go up to the lady and she starts talking very fast, looking at a second older lady that she's with. She's explaining something complex, because she's waving her arms and pointing in various directions. Now is the time for me to announce, "Lady, I don't really speak Spanish."

But they keep talking—thinking maybe that I am embarrassed or ashamed when what I am is clueless—as I stand here, shaking my head and shrugging my shoulders, until suddenly the older lady gets a look at my legs.

"*Aie*!" she cries. Her companion—the younger woman—says (in English), "What are you wearing?"

"A kilt," I tell them.

"*Que*?" says the older lady.

"I'm in a pipe band," I tell them.

"What?"

Inner Mack speaks up: *Dude, use google translate.*

I put my finger up, take out my smart phone.

"*Gaitas*," I tell them.

They look at each other and then ... they chortle. The younger one hushes the older one, clears her throat and says, "Are you visiting from Scotland?"

"I'm from San Dimas, California," I tell them. The two women look at each other and converse. I think but am not sure I hear the words "Bill and Ted" mixed into the exchange. They start giggling in earnest.

I'm getting pissed off at this point, but Inner Mack says:

Dude, do you want these two ladies to tell their families about this young sort of possibly Latinx guy at the train station and WHAT A COMPLETELY IMPOLITE AND DISRESPECTFUL ASSHOLE HE WAS?

So I keep on standing there. Breathe.

The younger woman finally says, "You're Mexican and wearing this and playing those?!"

"Salvadorian," I tell her. "Like a quarter. On my dad's side." They confer, and the older woman looks at me, says something.

"What's the matter with you that you don't speak Spanish?" the younger woman translates.

"*Es un idioma hermoso!*" the older woman adds, wagging her finger at me. "*La gente cultivada habla español!*"

I took French 1 and 2 in college and so I understand enough to figure out that I'm not as cultivada as I should be because if I were, I'd have cultivada'ed language skills in the *Español* department. So, I bow to them like any cultivated Highlander would after talking to ladies and walk back to my place in line.

The ladies grab another passerby and they all start speaking Spanish about something.

They look back at me, as the older lady points at my legs.

They all start laughing again.

It's my turn at the ticket window, and guess what? The girl at the window is cute. I mean not gorgeous, not model-hot, but still nice.

I like nice. I can't see much of her, but—you know—sometimes you have a feeling about someone?

Inner Mack warns, *Watch out—the good feeling you had about someone didn't work out last time*.

I proceed with caution and tell her where I'm going and ask whether I want *Merveilleux Bienvenue* or *Merveilleux Centre-Ville* and she tells me that I want *Merveilleux Bienvenue*, and then she suggests that maybe I want to get on the next train at 10:30 a.m. It's this special fancy vintage train that's really scenic and has gourmet food.

She smiles nicely with quite good teeth, so I explain about how I'm a teacher in training, and I don't have a lot of extra cash, but my recently deceased dad told me I should take the train cross-country once in my life, and to stop off in Narrow Interior because it was a cool town with a mysterious history.

It isn't, but I don't say that part.

The ticket girl keeps smiling.

"You can get a second-class ticket," she says, "and even if the train is crowded you'll have to stand for just a little while," and now she leans over the counter with her forehead pressing against the glass separator. "People get on and off the train all the time, and for sure a seat will open up by the first stop if you can't find one before that. And you get to ride to the border on an amazing old-school train that looks like that fancy one in *Murder on the Orient—*"

I interrupt her—which is not one of my best qualities. My ex-girlfriend says this is one of the many small but asshole-ish things that I do during the course of an average day.

But I want to call her attention to my kilt! So I carry on with my interruption.

"Even if I have to stand up, I guess that way my kilt won't get wrinkled," I say brightly. "Brightly," because I've noticed that something that girls like is when you really try to make a positive interpretation of things. My ex said I was always so negative and that was such a surprise, because when she met me, she thought I was so cheerful and really into feminist film theory in a happy go lucky kind of way and that's what she liked best about me. Then she found out that first impression was completely wrong.

So … I'm trying to learn from my mistakes. Or else I'm repeating them. But I'll only be repeating them if I can't keep up the good work of being positive during this conversation.

Interesting challenge, says Inner Mack. *How about your trying to remain positive for the entire trip?*

I can't respond to that challenge currently, because I am explaining about why pipe bands are cool and how I've lately started practicing the San Dimas Serene Awareness™ breathing technique and how it has absolutely changed my life for the better (despite the facts [which I do not mention] that I had to quit my Film Studies Graduate Program where everyone hated me [because of my ex] and change schools and do a credential program where the other students like me fine pretty much, but the program director wonders if I'm really suited for this type of teaching, because to quote her I'm awfully "thinky"; how I am still in school at 30; and am also still sleeping on my mom's couch until I graduate and get a full-time teaching gig).

"Can you hurry the fuck up?" says someone in back of me. Not Mr. Scowly Weird Flag Guy. Some girl behind him. I step back and turn, but I can't see who's talking, so I turn back to the information/ticket girl, who is beaming at me. Which I always take as an encouraging sign.

"Wow," she says (at last!). "I love your kilt!"

Yay!

I explain to her (and anyone listening [potential pipe banders may be in line and just haven't changed into their gear yet]) about the history of the kilt and how my particular kilt is related to an actual RELATIVE of mine on my mother's side, and that I do indeed have a lineage going back to the Royal Stewart tartan (we were lesser Stewarts of course, but still it's pretty cool), and how the family recalls the subjugation of the Scottish people by the British.

"Like in *Outlander*!" the ticket girl says, and Inner Mack says: *Ok, granted—that show is really stupid, but you are not going to say that. Instead, you're going to **stay positive** and get her email and see if somehow you can connect with her when you come back through on the way home when—*

"For Christ's sake!" says that bitchy girl voice somewhere in back of Flag Guy.

I pause and look back around more successfully because Flag Guy has bent over to tie his shoe. I look past three more relatively normal looking people.

I see four girls standing together.

The complainer keeps complaining to the other three, and, not to put too fine a point on it, she is not soft-spoken, she is not tall, not unskinny, and she is not a nonsmoker. She's puffing away on an actual cig with her black hair, petite tight black jeans, black crossbody messenger bag and Doc Martens boots, and she looks like she could be a tiny type of goth, although her black t-shirt reads a nerd message if ever there was one: CEPHALOPOD POWER.

Smoking killed my dad so I'm not a fan to begin with, and she's talking to her girlfriends in a very loud voice about how slow this all is, and why are the machines broken, and she doesn't want to go to Canada, but her parents are making her.

The other three are laughing really loud, and then getting very serious, and one even starts crying while another says, "Quirk, first your octopus tattoo just disappears, and now all of you is going to disappear. We are going to miss you so much! We HATE that you are moving to Canada."

The loud smoking tiny goth one—Quirk?—starts to sing, and—I'm not kidding—she embarks on a completely terrible rendition of Frank Sinatra's "My Way." In the meantime, the other three girls are nodding and swaying to the music and looking pissed off and privileged in those broken-down dresses that you know cost a bundle. Just from the way they stand there in those misshapen sacks of faded material, you can see that they have this *thing*—rich people have it, and white people really have it too, and rich white girls *really* have it—like they own the world so completely, they don't even have to act like they care about it. And it's an inferior world, come to think of it, and they are in the process of ordering up a new one.

I'm thinking about striding past the Flag Guy and just telling these girls that they just have to effing wait their turn, and not act like such private school bitches (which you can just kind of TELL they are), and to please stop ruining Sinatra (who was a GREAT singer and a seriously cool guy), and by "cephalopod" does she mean "octopus"? when one friend of the goth-complainer-smoker interrupts:

"Look!" she says. "There's a first-class ticket window right there."

"Aren't there five of them that just opened up?" says the second smallest of the four.

"No, silly," says mini-goth. "There's just the one. You must still be tripping."

"Do you wear your kilt all the time?" says the quite cute ticket counter girl.

I turn back to her as she gives me my ticket and my change.

"Absolutely," I say. "Kilts are much more comfortable than pants, although there is an issue with pockets and where you put your wallet."

The ticket girl giggles at that one. I lean my elbow on the window, and I'm just about to tell her how a true Scotsman wears a sporran on his belt to hold his car keys and stuff when Scary Flag Guy pokes me in the back.

"We ain't got all day," he shouts into my ear.

When I turn around to face him, I do in fact notice that the line behind me is beginning to get kind of long despite the fact that the quite tiny smoking goth girl has gone off with her friends.

But I need a little more time!

"Just a moment, please sir," I say with my teacher in training authority voice and then I grin at him because he actually looks like he could be a decent person if he could stop scowling and kind of hunching his shoulders in a way that's weirdly threatening. And also if he used some teeth whitener. I don't care what anyone says: having white teeth makes SUCH a difference in how a person looks. It's why I brush regularly and use those strips.

Then I turn back to the girl at the counter. "It's a delicate balance," I say to gain a little time, because I don't like to be pressured and it makes me nervous when I'm pressured, and then I have to slow myself down again.

"What is?" says the ticket girl.

"Being in a pipe band is," I say. My ex said my stories were too long, but you know, you need the detail to get a feel for what's at stake in a story or what is truly involved in an explanation, which is why in my opinion the early Wim Wenders films are terribly underestimated. I keep on explaining this notion of visual exactitude—as well as the concept of the road movie as an epic—to my teaching supervisor, whenever she tells me my lesson plans are too complicated for high school students.

I lean my elbow back on the counter, which isn't easy to do because the counter is very narrow and I'm over six feet so I have to hunch a little, but I'm doing it because it's a debonair move if you can make it work. Like Pedro Pascal does in *The Mandalorian,* only taller with a face you can see and a kilt.

"You have to be pretty physically strong to work bagpipes," I say to the ticket counter girl. "It takes a lot of lung power, and the bag is also pretty heavy, so you have to have strong shoulders, and legs. And maintaining the equipment isn't—"

Upside Down American Flag pokes my shoulder AGAIN.

I turn around AGAIN.

"Hurry it up!" says the guy. "Or I'll—" He raises his arm and makes a fist.

Oh, how I'd like to—

Don't lose your temper, Inner Mack says. *Deploy Pedagogy 101 technique A STAT.*

San Dimas Serene Awareness™ Cleansing Breath.

"Just a second!" I say to Flag Guy. I gaze at him at him with sudden wonder and admiration. "You know, you look a lot like the guy in *Highlander*!"

"What?" he says. He puts his fist down.

Ok, just between you and me—he doesn't look anything like the immortal warrior Connor MacLeod. On the other hand, he seems super-angry like those guys in *Highlander*, and I can't help but visualize him standing up and yelling THERE CAN BE ONLY ONE right here in the train station. And I seriously think it would make him feel better if he could get in touch with those feelings by projecting them onto an iconic and very masculine fictional persona.

Continue talking, says Inner Mack. *Connect meaningfully with a potentially disruptive student.*

"Of course, I don't mean you look like the *actor*," I reassure him, because I bet he wouldn't like to look like Christopher Lambert, who played a lot of crappy parts in pretty sucky movies like that terrible *Tarzan* movie. "I mean you look like the *character*."

I smile at him, and he squints a little because my smile is especially brilliant because—getting ready for the trip—I just had my teeth cleaned by Marilyn herself of Claremont Organic Teeth Cleanings R Us.

The future Highlander opens his mouth to say something.

"Ok—thanks—NEXT," shouts the ticket window girl.

I smile again—brilliantly—and step out of the line.

I walk off briskly to find my train track. I adjust my kilt. You know, the world would be a better place if more people were in pipe bands, or at least knew more about Scottish history and stuff. Guys especially. I mean when you don't have role models in real life, you have to look to—

That's when I remember, I didn't get that girl's email. Or even her name.

Dude, says Inner Mack. *You have to take ACTION with women.*

I DO or at least I MEAN to, but then THINGS HAPPEN, and then somehow ... the chance passes me by.

"You're too passive, Mack," my sister says, which is rich coming from someone who is like in year 10 of trying to get her Ph.D. in counseling.

As I'm thinking this, goth smoker girl comes up to me.

"I need to tell you that you're a real asshole," she says. "I saw you mocking me and my friends while you stood there trying to hook up with that girl at the ticket window!"

"I was just being friendly," I say back to her. "You know, it wouldn't kill you to be nice."

"Maybe it WOULD kill me," she interrupts. "Everyone wants short girls to be nice so they can say, 'Well, she's petite and sweet.'"

"You can count on my NEVER thinking that you are sweet," I say back, which I think is pretty fast thinking on my feet. But she just leans into me, turning her face up, and as she does, her whole face flashes a brilliant dark blue.

"And by the way kilt-boy, *Highlander*Con is in Toronto next month, not Merveilleux City," she says.

"I'm not—"

But she has already turned on her heel and is walking back to her tittering friends in their over-priced bag-dresses. The air around her swirls with a blueish aura, and just for a second, I see suctioned arms waving from her shoulders.

Well, damn, how did she know about *Highlander*Con?

Whatever. Why can't the women I meet be like Elizabeth Taylor in *Butterfield 8*? All badass and sexual (at least until the censors take over the second half of the film and the director has Liz drive off a cliff). I could fall in love with *her*.

Or if I'm going to meet a woman on a classic train, what about what's her name ... Eva Marie Saint on the train with Cary Grant in that Hitchcock movie? I could fall in love with her too. She's an undercover agent, working to thwart the bad guys.

My dad was crazy for that one, despite the fact that my Film Studies professor felt that *North by Northwest* was one of Hitchcock's less inventive films.

2

Diamond Williams does not want to be the heroine of the oldest story

It's the oldest story, and that's weird. Being a poet, the imagery and language of my life should be shiny and striking. Shattering, even.

But this story of my life doesn't merit lyricism. It's so cliché, it's like a soap opera, only boring.

He's a professor. He's *my* professor. Russell is my mentor, actually. Creative Writing. Master of Fine Arts program. He's a little bit famous. He's not a lot older. He's married. I'm not. He's white, of course. Yes, there are people of color in power at the University, but still not that many. He has power. He has influence.

People say he's a great writer. I don't know. But he's a wonderful editor, that's for sure. And he's encouraging, always.

He builds me up. He gives me confidence.

I'm from Tennessee.

I'm here because I got the fellowship. Not just a fellowship. The big one.

But truth is, the fellowship makes things weird. It made the other students in the program kind of glide away because they thought I thought I was all that, not just because I'm Black, but also because I'm older. I tried to be especially nice, and it only isolated me further. Just me and my fellowship.

The fellowship means I don't teach. Which is great. Only, I don't get any teaching experience. That's a weird catch. That means whatever job I get has to be based on my publications, and I don't have big or important ones; I've just got poems published in the university creative writing magazine.

He said he'd help me, because publishing is so racist.

He's handsome, he's lived in Africa. He's lived in Norway. He's been mentioned for big prizes and he keeps on almost getting them. He's up for a grant from the National Endowment for the Arts. He's been on NPR, he was on PBS last week.

He said I was pretty.

My writing has gotten better.

He said he would help me and he has. I get grants to do this, grants to do that. I get slots at bookstores and little conferences.

Now we are on the way to Merveilleux City to the big writing conference and the small gem-like publishers who favor literature. And to where the jobs are, such as they are, in Creative Writing, English and related fields.

He said he loved me, a couple of months ago.

Do I love him? A sliver of me does. But there's precious little room for emotion in the space I inhabit.

We ducked into the bathroom off the observation car once we got on the train, and we've been switching between the bathroom and the observation car ever since. As second-class passengers we don't get fancy compartment seating, so for privacy we use the bathroom.

Not for sex, although we do sex and sex is good. No, the bathroom on the train is for editing. We read our work to each other, and we like to do that in private where no one can hear. His idea. He says, "Diamond, we work best when art feels like a transgression, a secret we will eventually leak out into the world."

Why so many secrets?

My friend DanieLa, who dropped out of the program and works at Bloomingdale's, says she wonders if he likes me also because I don't act Black, don't talk Black either, so that's confusing and also safe. I hate that she said that, but I think that's why a lot of men—who aren't Black—have liked me. I spent a year in Geneva, and I slept with men who were German, Egyptian, Persian, and Chilean. They all said, "You're very sophisticated."

I think they meant white-sounding.

"You have already tried this, haven't you?" DanieLa said to me when I visited her in Portland last year. "You have been married twice already. Both men white. Trying to escape Memphis? Trying to escape the family?"

If DanieLa were here, she'd say to me:

"Just write, sis. You're really good."

But I'm getting ready to graduate, my fellowship is ending, and I haven't placed my poetry collection with a publisher. And I don't have a job.

He says he'll help me.

But something feels off today.

"We have to be a bit careful," he said when we got on the train. "The writing world is small. We might run into someone." Then he talked again about how he will introduce me to a particular publisher, someone who likes hybrid poetry. "Someone who will get your writing," he said.

We start to walk out of the bathroom after our first session of love and editing, but as he is unlocking the door and stops to kiss me, he almost walks right into this tiny white girl. She sees me, and I'm worried for a second that she will recognize Russell. Russell steps back into the bathroom and slides the door closed as the girl rushes past and into the observation car.

We wait a moment. This time I'm the one to slide the door open and close it behind me. I look up and down the hall. Coast is clear.

I tap on the door three times to let Russell know all is well. He taps back. Then I go to the observation car; he comes a moment later and we drink a couple of whiskeys. The car contains a small, fancy cocktail bar out of an old movie, and I can imagine myself as Lena Horne in a full-length gown getting my due at last. It quietens down; the few other passengers leave and then we're alone in the deep velvet banquettes, below the chandeliers tingling with the movement of the wheels. The barman goes off to do something. My professor puts his hands under my skirt, and the rocking of the train brings me someplace good. The barman comes back, and my professor taps my shoulder. We go back to the bathroom. This time we use a handicapped bathroom close to the bar. Since it's a bigger space, we can move and get into what is happening in the scene of his next book, where the hero is offstage at some musical event. I'm looking for atmosphere to put into the scene to make it feel just right.

"What's the image I'm looking for here?" Russell asks me. We kiss. We fool around. Time passes. We work more. Love more.

Eventually, we give up on the manuscript and go back for another drink.

We're sitting and someone says "excuse me" in a very loud voice.

It's that tiny white girl again! With a young guy this time. Wearing a kilt.

"Excuse me," repeats the white girl, who is actually kind of pretty now that I look at her, despite her gothy black hair and eyeliner. She has nice skin and large green eyes. "Do you remember the old guy I was with?"

Russell is sitting next to me, and he pokes my ribs.

"Ouch," I say. Then I get it.

"No," I say. "I haven't seen anyone."

"But didn't we literally (literally?) run into each other just a little while ago?" she asks.

"No," I say.

We get up and go back to the oversized bathroom.

"What was that all about?" I say to Russell. Meaning both the girl and his embarrassment.

"She saw us both together in the bathroom of a vintage luxury train," he says, "and people can be so racist. A white man and a Black woman, and one of them, well, quite well known. People talk."

"Are you worried about your wife?" I lean against the sink. I look good like that.

"I told you, Diamond—there may be others going to the conference on this train," he says. He looks at me. I look back. There's always a lot of heat in those looks.

It strikes me how he is able to smile in a way that is both admiring and—just a little—dismissive.

"I've just now texted Sergei over at ... Publications. He'll meet us for drinks, tonight. But we can't be late." He takes out a blunt and lights it, despite the no smoking placards in here. Puts it between his lips, and again, puts a hand on my left hip and then the other on my right.

"I'm going to the bar and write, and you join me when you're ready." He pulls back, adjusts his pants and shirt. Takes a drag. And puts the blunt between my lips. A suggestive move. It usually works. He smiles again.

"And babe, don't forget that reputation actually matters."

"What do you mean?" I ask.

"You're the difficult to please, avant-garde writing, older, gorgeous fellowship winner, aren't you, Diamond? Whereas I—"

He pauses and smiles again.

"I'm just an Armenian-American writer like William Saroyan. Making good and trying to help talented minority students."

"What are you trying to tell me, Russell?" I say, I stand up at my full height and when I do that I'm as tall as he is. With heels, taller.

He shakes his head, diminished. Then he looks at me, in full patient-yet-supportive-white-mentor mode.

"I'm just saying, remember—it's all about the book contract. And the connections you need to make and maintain to get another and another."

He smiles a different smile now. He has a lexicon of them. This smile looks like one of those anti-heroes in a B-movie from the 50's. That smile tells me I'm going to have to play ball, as they say.

He slides the door open and walks out. I look at myself in the mirror.

"It *is* all about the book contract," the mirror tells me. "With the contract you can get a university job and you can have health insurance and from there ... big success awaits. Another man too. Maybe."

"Who are you really, Russell?" I ask the mirror in the handicapped bathroom on the fancy train going to Québec.

Are you just another literary white man trying to do me a favor, as you hang on tight to your privilege, and somehow get credit for being an ally?

Why has leaving your wife not come up in the conversation lately?

I can't answer those questions. I stand in that big bathroom, balancing on my heels as the train surges forward. I remember that I'm a grad student. I have to get my degree and those good recommendations. Those personal connections make all the difference.

Like I said. It's the oldest story. But damn, I want to tell a new one.

3

Mack cannot help but help

We depart and I'm chugging along with my fellow bagpipers in a corner of a creaky old second-class car right next to what I guess is the kitchen area serving the dining room, because I can hear yelling, arguing, the clatter of pots and pans, and drawers and cabinets being opened and slammed shut. We are joking around playing old stuff like the Beatles greatest hits on bagpipes (which sound pretty good), and someone's eating a particularly gross-smelling tuna sandwich while someone else has fired up some weed, when she slides open the door to second class. The combination of pipes piping, smokers smoking and not such great tuna reeking hits her, I guess. The train swerves and she crumples against the hallway wall.

Who am I talking about?

That tiny but obnoxious goth Sinatra-singing smoking girl, of course.

I grab her arm to keep her from falling, and I can't help myself but ask her if she's ok.

"Forget it," she says, pulls her arm from my hand, and just proceeds with the crumpling.

I catch her, which isn't easy, because for someone who is kind of tiny she's—surprisingly—very hard to lift. But I manage it.

"Feeling faint?" I say, and then I explain as I'm trying to keep her from breaking her neck, "That happened to my dad a lot. He would just go wonky."

She sits down against the wall.

"I'm messed up," she says.

"That's obvious," I say. "Did you fall out of your black leather post-punk stroller as a child, and hit your head on the pavement?"

"No, smart-ass, I got hit on the head as I was getting on the train!" She pauses. "And then I must have fallen or something, because my ankle feels twisted. It's not working right."

"How can I help?" I say.

Why did I just say that?

You did this, Mack, because you do not want to be called an asshole by a girl ever again.

"Just leave me alone, man." Classy response.

"No—I can't do that," I say. "My mom always taught me to insist on helping strangers in trouble." I think for a minute. "Of course, that's how she ended up marrying my dad."

She looks at me like she can't quite believe I am as truly as idiotic as I sound.

"Who helped who?" she says. "Oh never mind."

She sits and looks at me. She has really giant green eyes. Like an anime character.

Talk to her, says Inner Mack. *She looks scared.*

"What's wrong?" I say.

"Ok—I'll tell you," she says. "Did you see an elderly guy with a red plaid scarf at the train station?"

I shake my head. "No. But there are a lot of old people around these days—they aren't very remarkable."

"He would have been on the platform too. Didn't you notice?"

"I only noticed you, and what a bitch you—"

"And you're an asshole. As I was TRYING to explain, this elderly man helped me on the train and bought me hot chocolate in the dining car. And now I can't find him."

"We haven't made any stops so he must still be on the train."

"Dummy—I KNOW that!"

"Calm down—no one is saying he isn't on the train."

"Dude—that's EXACTLY what everyone else is saying."

"Who's 'everyone'?"

"The conductor ticket-taker guy. Two waiters in the dining car and the maître d'. Other randos—I don't know who they are. They all insist they never saw him."

That does seem a bit weird. I decide to slide down to her level and sit next to her in the hallway.

"Let's go through it again. The old man helps you on the train, you get drinks in the dining car. Then what happens?"

"I closed my eyes for a little bit," she says, her voice getting quieter. "And when I opened them he wasn't there."

"A little bit?" I am trying not to be the asshole she thinks I am. But this girl does not exactly have her head on straight. "Are you sure about the time?"

"I wasn't looking at a clock," she replies sharply. So I look at my watch. It's been fifteen minutes since we left the station. This girl might have had her eyes closed for one minute, or five. She might have passed out over her hot chocolate. How out of it is she? I try to think like a detective and not an asshole. "Do you remember what you two talked about?"

"He asked me how I was. He talked about his family a bit, they're in Canada. He told me to rest. Oh, he told me his name. Gabriel."

Now we're getting somewhere. "Gabriel," I repeat. "Was that his first name or last name?"

"Yes," she mutters. "One of those."

I groan. "So then, this Mr. Gabriel—"

"Mr. Gabriel doesn't sound right," she adds. "Just ... Gabriel."

"OK," I say. "Just Gabriel helps you on the train and then disappears. And before that, you say you hit your head?"

"I just grazed it, although I did drop some acid last night."

"You did WHAT?"

"Are you going to help me or not?"

I'm about to just stand up and walk back to my bag pipes, but then I remember my ex Elizabeth saying, "You're never sympathetic when it matters. You're like Lawrence Olivier's Mr. Darcy in that terrible Hollywood adaptation of Jane Austen, only you aren't rich and you stay impossible."

Next, I think of the assignment I gave the middle schoolers I worked with last semester in La Verne. I told them to go home and interview their family members. And if they have a camera phone, to film the interview as well as write it up.

"You can learn all kinds of things, if you treat your family like strangers you want to learn about."

"They ARE strangers," said one kid. Still, they got a lot out of the interviewing process. And some of the movies were pretty good. Although my supervisor said this assignment was too complicated for sixth graders.

Stop with the internal dialogue, says Inner Mack.

"I know!" I say. "Let's interview everyone you've talked to since you got on the train."

"I thought you said you were going to be of actual help."

She's certainly a charmer, this girl.

"It'll be helpful if I come along because I have a way with people."

I can't tell whether she sighs or snorts, but I give her my hand, and she takes it and after some deep breathing, I manage to hoist her to her feet. How can someone so miniscule be so hard to lift?

"When you talk, you scare people," I add. "They probably thought you're in some debutante goth rock band and you wanted them to put you up or give you money."

"I'm not a g—hey, what's your name?"

"Mackinnon Macdonald Flores at your service. But you can call me Mack."

She raises her eyebrows.

"And you're Quirk, right?"

"Allison," she says. "Muth. Which means courage or spirit, F.Y.I."

"So what's Quirk?"

"That's what friends call me."

"Oh."

"Let's get going. These bagpipes are giving me a migraine."

I nod to a piper neighbor. He nods back, moving my bagpipes next to his.

I think of something. "Wait a minute," I say. "You're not a Film Studies major, are you?"

"Is that like fucking *auteur* theory and having to watch endless Truffaut?"

I guess that means no.

4

Mack exercises his charm on the passengers

We walk the narrow aisle of second class towards the first-class car at the front of the train. Allison lurches periodically, and I steady her by a discrete elbow grab.

"I'm fine!" she keeps on saying.

The first-class car is guarded by a sign etched into the window of the car door in frosted script:

RESTROOMS RESERVED FOR FIRST-CLASS PASSEN-GERS ONLY

I figure I'm not supposed to enter this car, but then again, I don't need to use the bathroom. I open the door, and the hallway widens and jogs to my right. On my left are fancy passenger compartments with glass windows and curtains. Some of the curtains are pulled, and I can't tell if anyone is inside. Other compartments have the curtains open to people sitting on roomy upholstered seats facing each other and looking out big picture windows. It all looks like something out of an old movie my father might watch on Turner Classic Movies, like *Twentieth Century* or—as the cute girl said at the ticket window—*Murder on the Orient Express.*

"Why are you watching these, Dad?" I asked him all the time. To be honest some of those films drove me crazy with their corny music and not archivally well-preserved black and white grainy visuals or else their over-bright colors that look like a commercial. Kubrick, they ain't.

"Movies about trains make me feel safe," he said. "Every train movie is an emotional journey. The journey always completes and a better world is discovered at the end."

He died on the sofa watching one of those old movies about crap that happened on a train. I don't remember the movie, but I remember the last scene. A woman opened her eyes, and the man said, "I feel as though you've been on a very long voyage."

My dad smiled at that. And then, he was gone.

"Wake up, Mackintosh," says Allison. "Time to use your way with people."

Sure enough, right ahead of us in the hallway is a tall guy talking seriously to an actual cowboy; he's wearing a cowboy hat with stars and moons on it and one of those shirts with the snaps, and he's even got a vest with fringe and a holster with a gun in it. Allison points at the cowboy, but the tall man seems less weird, so I try him first.

"Excuse me," I say, "this person says she's lost her friend."

"Yes," says the tall man, "we both heard from the conductor, some young woman hit her head and is saying that someone is missing. It's an interesting case. It reminds me of my tour in Afghanistan."

Case? Inner Mack says. *Afghanistan?*

"And you are the young woman?" says the tall man, extending his hand. That's when the cowboy jumps in.

"Hey there y'all. My name is Jimmy Shoulders, evangelical Christian rodeo star, and this here is my ball and chain and my little buckaroo." He gestures at the woman and small boy seated in the fancy vintage train compartment. The boy doesn't look like his father or mother at all; he looks like me. Adopted?

On the other hand, I'm from SoCal, so I know all about blended families. More importantly, the minute someone says "star," I know what I have to do.

"What a thrill to meet you, Mr. Shoulders," I say. "And what a good-looking kid! How old?"

"Nine. And the little lady in the corner is 'a course, Ms. Tiffany Tolliver."

I look at the woman sitting next to Mrs. Shoulders. She looks just like …

"You remember HER!" shouts Mr. Shoulders encouragingly. "She's the one who had herself made over so she could be a stunt double for the President's daughter. She worked at the White House, and she's on tour publicizing her new book!"

I incline my head. Tiffany Tolliver really does looks almost exactly like the second daughter of the former President. Blonde. Corners of mouth tucked in and upper lip pulled high, showing teeth. Shoulders in a kind of perpetual shrug. Skirt just a little too short.

"Hi there!" I say. "Did you know that the former President's eldest son was at the last convention I was at, judging most improved pipe band?"

Tiffany Tolliver doesn't look up from her tablet, but she does utter the following from behind clenched teeth as she watches what sounds like a press conference.

"Not former."

Oh, says Inner Mack. *She's one of those.*

"I should probably introduce myself as well," interjects the tall guy. "Although you might already recognize me," he adds, ducking his head.

I don't recognize him. He looks like an actor, which is to say he looks kind of like everyone, only better. But Allison is studying the tall guy carefully.

"Say," says Allison. "Aren't you?" I jab her in the ribs and shake my head at her, because she's being a bit rude. This is no way to conduct an interview! I had better take over.

I say, "Aren't you one of the Congressmen who lost their re-election last fall in some contested vote situation?"

Wild guess. But the (former) Congressman nods brightly at my question.

"Yes! Or rather no," he says, ducking his head again in a way that's supposed to look humble (politicians, honestly). "My opponent was seated, but almost immediately died of a sudden heart attack—such a tragedy—so there's a special election which I'm of course running in ... but the real reason I look familiar is because I've also done some television acting—"

"Right! What show?" asks Allison.

He replies, "You might remember I had the second lead in BOYS OVER BOUGAINVILLEA, PASADENA soap opera, which is a remake of the Korean drama—"

"Of course! I loved B.O.B.P.!" exclaims Allison. "Weren't you that melancholy violinist who the heroine almost ends up with?"

The Representative nods and grins. My God, his teeth are white.

"Yes, that was me! After college at Princeton, and before I served as a medic in Afghanistan, of course." He shrugs his shoulders. "And had several other notable roles and was involved with some exciting business ventures—oh, and please call me Joe."

I'm trying hard and mostly failing not to feel intimidated by this guy. Afghanistan AND Princeton? And acting? Jesus. Even Inner Mack is at a loss.

"Jeepers, Joe, why did you quit acting!" says Allison.

"Thanks for asking, that's really empathetic of you," he answers, leaning over her in a practiced and yet not overtly condescending way. "After the war, I felt that I needed to serve the country, and with my medical knowledge, I thought about med school, actually did a few years at Stanford while I played some amateur hockey, but then felt I could be of greater use in politics. You know, service to the community is everything, isn't it?"

With a herculean effort I stop myself from rolling my eyes. What bullshit.

Maybe not, warns Inner Mack. *What you have you done for the world lately?*

Allison gazes at him, transfixed. I study him too. He is so generically handsome, he looks like he's about to perform an aftershave commercial. But at the same time, I would be hard-pressed to describe what he looks like. His face is amorphous ... shifting ...

You know, it wouldn't kill you to shave more carefully and moisturize periodically, Inner Mack observes philosophically.

"What are you doing on a train, Mr. Congressman?" I ask, trying to get this interview back on track.

"Trains are the best way to meet the people," he said, as if I'm a trusted confidant and not some rando he's bumped into on the train. "And it's my ongoing interest in medicine—in particular, trauma—that has me travelling up to Moretz, just past Albany. Beautiful spot. Secluded, yet filled with enthusiastic voters, passionate about this country. My campaign headquarters happen to be up there too, right down the block from the medical center there—which has spectacular facilities. The docs up there have discovered a surgical means to remove trauma from the brain and I'm quite excited about that pioneering effort that will really improve the lives of our vets and will—"

"Speaking of trauma, Joe," interrupts Allison, ruining the easy conversational relationship that I was doing a pretty good job of building with the Congressman. "Did you happen to see my friend Gabriel, who's an elderly man?"

"Unfortunately, no," says Joe.

"Let me ask these ladies," I say, because I don't want to hear any more about the accomplishments of the Representative. I lean into the compartment. I figure I'll talk to Ms. (ex) Presidential Daughter Dead Ringer first.

"Your excellency," I say. "Have you seen my friend's friend?"

Tiffany Tolliver sighs and looks up from her tablet. "No, please stop bothering me, unless you wish to purchase a copy of my new bestselling memoir *ALMOST TIFFANY: How I Gave My Face for the First Family, Volume 1.*"

"I beg your pardon. And what about the lady next to you?"

Mrs. Shoulders looks at me blankly and I realize I have to change my mode of address.

"Did y'all happen to get a peek at the old feller my friend is jawing about?"

"Helllll nooooo," says the wife. "I ain't seen no varmint here that fits that there description."

I turn my attention back to the hallway. Sure enough, the Representative has taken over. "What do you remember about Mr. Gabriel?" he asks Allison. Grinning.

Allison smiles back at Joe, and then she wrinkles her brow so tightly I don't know how the skin doesn't just peel right back over her head. "He said he was a retired psychologist."

"What was he wearing?" I ask.

She looks at me, annoyed. "NOT a kilt."

I ignore that and look at Allison kindly but with expectation. My mom taught me that if people are rude to you, you need to be very sweet back to them, because either they respond positively or it makes them furious and they still have to try to respond positively.

Then the description comes.

"I don't remember a lot," Allison says. "But I *can* tell you that Gabriel was wearing black pants that were probably expensive, sensible black Rockport shoes—you know those ones with the fit flop technology but made for old people—teal Smartwool socks and a white Brooks Brothers shirt with narrow green stripes."

I shake my head. She can barely remember the guy's name, but she remembers his socks? But she's not through. "Grey tinged horn-rimmed glasses. Oh! And he was wearing hearing aids. He was also wearing a large ring with an amber stone in it, and a silver metal wristwatch and a silver chain bracelet over that. And he had a lovely red plaid scarf that he showed me for a moment because I was cold."

My ears perk up. "What kind of plaid?"

"Red," she says. "Like your kilt."

I stiffen. "I'll have you know that my kilt is not just any old plaid. It's a Royal Tartan."

Allison ignores my correction, and just keeps on going.

"Oh! And also, Jewish. He has the look."

"What look?"

"You know—the kindly Jewish gentleman look."

I shake my head. I have no idea what the hell she's talking about.

"Also—blue eyes. Slightly Asiatic."

"Huh?" This time it's the Representative who's not following.

"The eyes. One out of five or maybe it's ten Eastern Europeans have that because of the Mongolian conquests. Didn't you know that, Joe?"

"I did not," he says politely. "Did anyone else see you with this gentleman?"

Allison thinks some more. Her forehead unwrinkles and her eyes open, as though she were glimpsing another world—something far away and yet present—that we should be able to touch but can't. It's funny: when she does that she looks almost pretty. She looks like she's about 16. The Edison lights in the ceiling of the compartment create a halo around her. Pale blue.

"There was the waiter and the maître d'," she recalls. "And wait, I think there were these guys in suits sitting right across from us in the dining car. They were talking about money, so they are probably businessmen, or accountants."

"Why didn't you mention the accountants before?" I ask her.

There's a DINING CAR here? asks Inner Mack. My stomach growls in agreement with my inner self.

I say, "Let's go find them."

"May I accompany you?" says Joe. "I'm really interested in research on memory and cognition, in particular how it may impact our women vets. This might be a case worth referring to in the research that my reelection staff is doing for the Armed Services." He pauses and smiles at Allison. "This study might really help—you know, feminism!"

Allison smiles back. She has very nice teeth.

Seriously? Feminism is what the guys in the Film Studies MA program would trot out before they hit on some clueless undergrad in her first semester.

"Please come with us!" says Allison. "I mean, anything for science and feminism!"

5

May-Bel tries to find her seat

Hello dear viewers! This is May-Bel again, the Happy Train Vlogger. Hello to my husband! I wish you were here to share this experience.

People from China, please watch this vlog before you visit America. You will learn many important things.

Here is a good travel tip: if you talk to people in the United States, they will ask you what it is like to live in China. Their faces will be very serious when they ask this. Please do not be surprised. People in America think that everyone in China is unhappy and not free. Tip 2: Don't be confused when Americans like to talk a lot about "freedoms"; these are things Americans can do because the judges in America say it is a part of being free. For example: the judges say Americans can have as many guns as they want. But sometimes, these judges say when people are not free. For example, in some parts of the country, judges say you have to give birth if you are pregnant.

But back to guns! We have been here for three weeks and so far we have not seen any guns or even heard a gunshot. Except maybe in the movies or on TV. Of course, soldiers have guns, but we have not seen them. This is good! This means that visitors to the United States should not worry.

OK, enough advice! Now that we are on the train let's try to find our seat.

Look at this beautiful hallway with a thick carpet with a design on it. My feet feel like they are floating rather than walking. These little lamps against the side of the train alternate with big show windows. Viewers, the interior of our train looks a little like the Famous Seven Stars train in Japan. The walls are a deep wood color. Across from the windows, on the other side of the train, are the compartments. These are special first-class compartments, and I am fortunate that I have been assigned a seat here although, of course I would be perfectly content to sit in second class.

Hmm. Where is compartment H?

A B C D E F

And now a door to the next car ...

Oh. This car is very different than the last one. The carpet is gone. The windows are narrow and there is no hallway. Just an aisle to walk through. Everyone is sitting in narrow rows of two seats. There is smoke in the air in this car, and mostly men. Some are standing up and talking to others who are seated. The men standing up are wearing skirts! And they are playing instruments that are very loud! Let's use a voice translation app to help us ask some questions!

"What instrument are you playing?"

"Bagpipes."

This is so interesting. Bagpipes are an ancient instrument played in Scotland, which is part of the United Kingdom.

Let us say goodbye to the bagpipe players and try to find our seat in the next car down.

Oh good, this is better. This is the dining car.

Dear viewers, you can see that this part of the train looks just like the famous film *Murder on the Express to the East!* There are chandeliers on the ceiling! Look at the beautiful tables covered with white tablecloths. Everything here is white. The tables are set with shiny white plates and cloth napkins. We will come here later. Yes, it's too bad the food in this country is so sweet. There is so much sugar in everything. And no one shares their dish with another, and people eat by themselves. Strange! On the other hand, the plates of meat are very large and the vegetables are very good also. So, never fear, viewers! You will manage to eat just fine in the U.S.

Let's go down one more car and hope for clarification of the seating question.

Now I see a metal sign on the door that says: "Observation Car."

Let's go inside and observe!

Wow! Look at the beautiful glass roof, out of which you can see trees and sky! Too bad it's raining and there really aren't leaves on the trees yet. No flowers yet either, just grey fields. Well, it is winter in parts of China as well, so we mustn't complain!

More windows along the wall, and against these are very comfortable looking velvet sofas. A sign above the sofa reads "Cocktail Lounge." This is the place where travelers drink alcohol. There is a lot of drinking in the U.S., and again very strange, people drink by themselves. I think Americans are not as happy as they say, and drink to forget their worries.

But I myself am very happy to be in such a beautiful train car with such representative scenery. Let's sit down and order a cup of coffee. Viewers, trust me: don't bother asking for tea in America. You get better tea on China Air.

6

Mack continues to charm but it's growing increasingly difficult

"Wait," Allison says. "There *was* someone else who saw Gabriel. A woman. And a man. They were in the bathroom together."

Joe nods thoughtfully, and I just raise my eyes to the ceiling. Sex on a train? What IS it with people wanting to have sex in strange awkward places? Even the young Japanese couple travelling to Memphis on *Mystery Train* don't do that. They're too busy experiencing the strangeness of the Deep South and looking for connections to Elvis Presley to have sex in such an uncomfortable manner.

(My dad hated that movie. "How the hell did THIS get on Turner Classic Movies?" he asked. [I liked it {dir. Jim Jarmusch}]).

"You don't ever want to do anything exciting," Elizabeth said to me a month before we broke up. We had just come back from the beach.

"You try getting all that sand out of your private parts driving through the traffic on Ventura Highway," I retorted, as we packed up our picnic things at Zuma and I folded up the blanket at around 11:30 a.m. I like to arrive early and leave early—to avoid the crowds.

"You win, Mack," she said. She knew I was right. But soon after that she took up with that obnoxious linguistics pedagogy guy from Huntington Beach.

So instead of making a snarky comment back to Allison about sexual activity on a train, I say, "Good! Now we're getting somewhere."

"Describe them please, Ms. ..." says the Representative.

"Muth," says Allison. "Like 'truth.' Anyhow, the woman—she was tall and quite beautiful with braids—maybe in her late 30's—and he was a bit older and tall as well. Um, he's white and she's Black."

We head down through the next car in search of the interracial couple. This is the second-class car with my would-be Scottish buddies, and I take a look to see that my bagpipes are still where I left them. Past second class is the dining car, where trendy aromas creep towards us from the blazing copper pans of an open kitchen: shallot, saffron, balsamic vinegar. I'm thinking that a vintage train should serve historically accurate cuisine. *Would you prefer a fish with all its bones and its head still on staring back at you?* Inner Mack inquires.

Good point.

Past the kitchen are rows of tables seating four people at most. The tables are covered in white linen, and there's a little Tiffany lamp at the end of each table. This must be where Allison had her drink with Gabriel ... or maybe just with herself. The tables are empty now.

The final car is an "observation car"—all glass—but it's also a café and bar with people sitting on velvet sofas and drinking cocktails and tea and stuff.

Damn, Inner Mack observes. *Are you in the wrong part of the train.* The cute girl at the ticket window wasn't kidding when she said the train was fancy.

As we walk in, an older man in a suit and tie looks up from his paperwork. He squints at us through his glasses and looks down at my legs. "You look ridiculous, young man," he tells me imperiously, and waves his hand while shaking his head in disapproval. Then he sighs loudly and begins to write on a legal pad with an enormous pen that looks like it's made of solid gold. A waiter arrives at his elbow with not one but two oversized martinis.

I look at Allison. She shakes her head. Clearly, not Gabriel.

The waiter looks up briefly at us. "*Bienvenu au Café Poulpe*. Someone will be with you *directement*." We turn our gaze from the rich old guy and his martinis and—bingo, there's a beautiful Black woman with braids sitting with this just-ok-looking white guy.

"Excuse me," I say to them. "Did you happen to see this person," I indicate Allison, "in the company of an elderly white gentleman wearing horn-rimmed glasses?"

The woman—did I mention she's beautiful?—opens her mouth to say something but the man speaks up right away.

"I'm afraid we haven't."

"Thank you very much—" begins the Representative, but Allison is not finished.

"That's not true," says Allison, who evidently has no sense of shame, so it's a good thing we are with her, because she's so weirdly brash that no one would even talk to her otherwise. She points to the man. "You saw us earlier when we were getting on the train."

Happily, they don't seem to understand what she is getting at.

"No," says the man. "I didn't see."

"You did too!" Allison says. Her brain fog seems to be gone now. "The two of you were in the bathroom and you opened the door and practically walked right into me."

"That's not what happened," the man says.

Allison leans over the couple, swings her leg and puts her foot on the armrest of the fancy sofa (WTF?).

"I don't know why you're lying unless you were having sex in the bathroom and you're worried what people are going to think. Well, guess what? No one cares. And if you're having sex on a train, well good for you, because sex on the train is probably amazing although I've never tried it personally. The point is not the sex."

I facepalm. Jesus. I try to interrupt, but she barrels ahead.

"The point is—my new old friend Gabriel, who has disappeared. I *know* Gabriel is somewhere on this train and I'm going to find him if I have to pound on the door of every bathroom you two or anybody else is in as you explore the lesser known regions of your sexuality. I need to find out what the hell happened to him."

Allison removes her foot from the armrest. "So thanks for nothing, you liars."

The man stands up. He towers over Allison, who glares up at him.

"I'm sorry but you are making a mistake." His tone makes it clear HE is not making a mistake. "The first time I saw you was here in the observation car a few minutes ago, when you stumbled in asking about your older friend with the red plaid scarf." He leans over his companion, taking her hand. "Shall we discuss what order the writers should go in for the panel on African Diasporic Contemporary Poetics?"

"Oy," says Allison. "PROFESSORS." She turns to me and the Representative. "Let's go."

"Does she always talk like this?" the Representative whispers to me. I nod, trying my best to NOT look sort of semi-delighted by Allison's ad hoc demonstration of determined baddassery. Joe pauses with the couple to make an explanation to the Professor that I can't hear exactly. Maybe he's campaigning. That's when I notice two serious-looking guys in cheap but formal suits sitting two rows down from the alleged bathroom sex couple.

"Look!" shouts Allison. "The accountants!"

They don't look up, so she bounds over to them. Then says "fuck" because apparently she forgot she'd hurt her ankle. She falls into them. They grab their drinks. All she does is crunch into the cocktail table, which—happily—is bolted to the floor of the train car.

At this point I think I'd better take over again, since the Representative is still back there apologizing to the Professor for the young lady's "antics," and explaining to them that he suspects some kind of secondary and tertiary trauma, because he's a vet and by the way do they happen to know what congressional district they live in?

Or maybe he's just thinking it. I hear people's thoughts sometimes.

Are you sure? Inner Mack wonders. *Or is what you hear just your own projection?*

I pull Allison back to her feet and I make first contact with the guys.

"Excuse me, can you help us?" I say to them.

"How?" says one of the accountants. He's wearing a truly ugly newspaper boy cap on top of what is probably one of the worst-made suits I have ever seen. If he's really an accountant, I can't imagine the business he could account for.

"I was drinking hot chocolate in the dining car with an elderly gentleman, and I asked for your table-setting—do you remember?" Allison says.

"Well, mate," says the second guy, who has really big ears and a cockney accent, "Sayid and myself—we were deep in conversation." Sayid nods.

"But you must remember us!" says Allison.

"I remember passing the table setting," says the guy with the newspaper boy cap, "but we were very involved discussing professional wrestling."

"Are you kidding?" Allison explodes. "Wrestling doesn't make you not notice *real* people!"

The big eared guy turns red. His face contorts into a truly scary monster expression. But his voice is measured.

"If that's what you think of the art form, then there's nothing left to be said."

"Let's not waste another moment talking to these people, Adrian," says Cap. "Let's get a refill on our drinks."

"Did she just imply that pro wrestling is fake?" says Ears. "Can you believe the nerve?" They stomp off.

"Nice work, Inspector Poirot," I say to Allison. "We should have said we were looking for The Rock."

"This doesn't make any sense. Why doesn't anyone remember Gabriel?" Allison says, ignoring my quite clever wrestling reference.

"Actually, this situation does make sense, if you consider the facts," says Joe the Congressman, who has caught up with us after securing the Professor's vote for this and all upcoming elections. "You mentioned you had taken LSD a few hours before boarding the train?"

"I don't remember telling you that," Allison says.

"This is precisely my point," says the Representative, "Even coming 'down' as they say from an LSD experience, certain lapses in memory happen because of the bonding to serotonin receptors in the brain which lights everything up, as well of course as the famous hallucinations that one has under the influence of such drugs."

"But I remember what Gabriel and I talked about and I remember everything about him!" Allison explains.

I'm silent because she was pretty loopy at the train station. And on the train just a few minutes ago.

Don't remind her about singing Sinatra, warns Inner Mack. *And how she turned blue for a second. Actually—she has done that a couple of times.*

Then Allison does something that really surprises me. She bursts into tears.

"Don't be afraid," says the Representative to Allison, and he takes her arm in a comforting way. "These effects are completely normal, and you will be just fine. You should relax, try to stay a bit quiet, drink a lot of liquids of course, as it will help to flush the rest of the drug out of your system, and—"

The loudspeaker makes one of those always incomprehensible announcements.

"Ah!" says the Representative. "We are stopping at a station; I'd love to jump out and grab a local newspaper. I always like to inform myself about what different American towns are concerned about. If you will excuse me," he adds. "Don't worry. You'll be just fine in a bit."

He walks back down the train car.

Allison grabs a cocktail napkin from one of the tables and blows her nose.

"Did I really tell him I was on acid?" she says to me. "I got so excited when I realized who he was that I have no idea what I said to him."

"I don't remember," I say. "Maybe." But she's not listening to me because she's already gotten a new idea.

"Hey," says Allison. "If this is the first stop then maybe Gabriel will get off from like the dining room or one of the bathrooms. Maybe he's—I don't know—masturbating or something."

"You said he was old!"

"Well, old people have to jerk off too," she answers, and I think to myself that that is actually a pretty good point.

"We can look out windows on both sides of the train and see if he like gets off here." Then she cuts me off. "STOP looking at me like I'm weird."

"You *are* weird," I say, "but what I *was* going to say—before I was so rudely interrupted—is that it seems strange to me that Representative Joe—and what is his last name anyway—is getting off the train to get a paper. He can just check his phone, right? Right?"

"The cell phone service is terrible on the train, and maybe he's just really interested in supporting the local paper. As a congressperson isn't he supposed to—you know—shop local and think global?"

Again, that's actually also not a terrible point. Allison's oddly perceptive at moments.

"Stop dreaming," says Allison. "Let's get into position!"

7

Mack gazes out of the train window with Allison

We walk back to the second-class car, past where the bagpipers are now playing Henry Mancini movie themes, as the train pulls into a station. In the middle of the car are rows of empty seats. The windows on both sides of this car are open part way down. I stick my head out a window facing the station, and Allison does likewise on the other side of the train.

To my right, I see the Representative bound off the train. Far to my left, a woman gets off the train as well. Long blonde hair. I see no sign of an old man, but there are plenty of people on the platform waiting to get on. Might one of these people be Gabriel? I look for a plaid scarf, and I don't see one of those either.

This does not seem to be a productive posture, says Inner Mack, and I have to agree, there's nothing to see on this train platform. I look for Representative Joe and find him showing not one but two newspapers to someone who looks a lot like Tiffany. She lights a cigarette (gross!

I hate people who smoke) and waves her hands at the Representative. Then they both get on their cell phones and head back to the train.

Wait! Now I DO see an actual old guy walking to the train. What direction did he come from? He's wearing a trench coat, brown leather gloves and a grey wig with bangs, and the wig is so big it makes the head inside look tiny. But he's not wearing a scarf, let alone one sporting a plaid of any kind. Still ... could this be Gabriel? He clearly doesn't match Allison's description, but she was so addled when she met Gabriel, she may not be remembering him clearly.

It's interesting you continue to dismiss Allison's perceptions, Inner Mack observes. Maybe. But at this point, I think I'd settle for finding just about any old man. I'd just like to get this thing resolved. So I can go back to ... my bagpipes.

The train starts up again.

8

Diamond confronts Russell

I want to know why you lied to that girl. You told her the first time you saw her was in the observation car. You saw her earlier, when we tried to exit the bathroom together. Are you telling the truth about never seeing her and the old man together?

Who cares if she's pathetic?

I want to know why you're always equivocating about everything.

I want to know why for all your leftist politics you never stand up to anyone in the department or publicly stand up for any student at a meeting.

I want to know why you're constantly critiquing and deconstructing at dinner parties, but you haven't shown up at a single demonstration since the women's march.

I want to know why you ordered and bought the BLACK LIVES MATTER bumper sticker, but then you removed it as soon as you got pulled over by the cops for speeding on a country road.

I want to know why you won't declare what it is we're doing in this thing called a relationship and I want to know why you haven't moved out of your house.

I want to know why I am fucking you AND editing your work for no good reason other than that you seemed pretty nice, are a more than average editor, and you're a semi-famous writer. But are we in love or not and if not then WHY am I continually listening to you read me your rough drafts out loud? That—I don't have time for.

Finally, I want to know why all your favorite writers are white men and why three of five writers you nominate for awards are white men.

Yes, I'm keeping count. Yes, I'm tracking it.

9

Mack receives good news

Allison and I meet back up in the hallway and the cowboy comes bouncing up to us.

"Well, what do all y'all know!" He leans a meaty arm on the wall and beams at us. "The little lady's friend done plum turned up. We've got him right where he darned well ought to be, in our fancy lil' compartment."

"What are you talking about?" Allison asks.

"Well I don't rightly know where's he's been to, but he sure as shootin' hasn't gotten himself beat up or hurt or kilt and he hasn't bit the dust on his own the way the old fellers do with them there heart attacks and strokes or havin' what my grandma called 'a spell' and fallen off the gosh darned train or kilt himself because being old is pretty darned depressing and maybe he's like that friend of my mama's whose dad didn't want to get any more decrepit than he was already so he just shot himself with a shotgun and rigged it all so the descendants would find him just stretched out a bleeding mess lying there with his head blown open in front of his station wagon. Anyhoo ... your little old man is sitting right there big as life and twice as natural so y'all go find him now, and don't keep jawing."

He turns and swaggers down the hall.

Performers.

10

Mack thinks, yes! And, no!

"This is great!" I say, and then I—without any warning—hug Allison. I don't know why I do that.

You know why, says Inner Mack. But I do my best to ignore him. She's not my type. I'm just ... glad for her. I'm glad she wasn't imagining things.

"Problem solved!" I say into her ear.

Now I'm noticing that she's a surprisingly good hugger. She doesn't stiffen or do the shoulders only hug, where the rest of your body levers away. She really hugs me back, even though what I did was surprising. It's a warm hug. It has a kinetic kindness to it. And as I rest for a moment inside this embrace, it feels like more than two arms encircle my waist and back. I am being held by a woman who is so complete and so multifaceted that her arms are everywhere holding me completely, lifting me up. Suctioning up my self-doubt and even my need to criticize things. Imbuing me with ... grace.

Then I pull back. Her small ear is pretty. Like a pink seashell.

She nods, takes a deep breath and smiles. The air around her shimmers blue.

"I feel cheerful now," she says. "Because I'm not crazy or tripping and I'm relieved Gabriel hasn't had a heart attack or a stroke or whatever because—Mack—he was so kind to me when I was messed up for no other reason than he wanted to be kind and that's such a rare cool thing—"

"I'm glad too," I say. But I also—feel—just a little bit—sad. I thought I couldn't wait for my adventure with Allison to end, and now here I am. Hoping it might go on a little longer.

My dad said that was the worst part about train movies. "The journey ends on a good note," he said at the end of *Von Ryan's Express*, "but not everyone makes it to the end together."

Hey, Sinatra is in that, isn't he?

We follow Jimmy back to his compartment in first class. I don't see the Representative anywhere. But the cowboy's wife and the probably adopted son are exactly where we left them, and Tiffany the former President's Daughter look-alike has taken her old seat and is still on her tablet. And there's the man with the grey wig I saw on the platform earlier, sitting opposite from Tiffany. He's smiling. This is Gabriel? I take a good look at his face, and despite myself, my heart lifts for a moment.

Grandfather, intones Inner Mack.

It's true and extremely weird: if you could strip this old man from his too-big wig, he'd look almost exactly like my grandfather, whom I never knew but just saw in pictures. My dad's dad, my Salvadorian grandfather. These old guys—they can be cool. They tell amazing stories, and it seems like they accomplished a lot with very little. It was a time when you could still be a hero, and have your family look up to you and think you were amazing and they somehow escaped this toxic masculinity that seems to circulate like a virus and that escape is such a cool thing and I'm thinking—

"That's not Gabriel," Allison says to me.

"Not Gabriel?" I repeat, kind of numbly.

"*Nyet*," says the old man. "I am Vladimir Tirtov."

"Have you ever seen her before?" I press him, pointing at Allison.

"Nyet," says Tirtov, spitting out the "t" this time. "I do not consort with young strange American girls."

Well, he sure isn't Salvadorian. Why did I think he looked like my—

"I *tell* you it's not him!" Allison says again, pointing at Tirtov the way a docent would point at a figure in a natural history diorama. "This man is a hostile Russian wearing a weird ascot with a pearl in it. And a turquoise ring and a Beatles wig!"

And oh my God, she's right. It IS a Beatles wig, circa 1966 *Rubber Soul*, only grey and too big. But Mr. Tirtov takes umbrage. "Young lady, I'll have you know that this wig was fitted especially for me by Kopf und Kopf in Germany. And my pearl pin was left to me by my mother, the grand duchess of Westphalia. As for my ring, it was given to me by the Navajo nation."

The Representative appears. "What is happening?" he asks.

"We found an old guy who isn't Gabriel," I tell him, making a long story short.

Tiffany Tolliver stops listening to the former president's speech on her tablet and puts a gloved hand to her forehead. "I never said he was Gabriel," she says slowly, enunciating every word. "You are all witness to this. I will not permit myself to be the victim of fake news or dragged into a Congressional inquiry." She bows her head reverently towards Vladimir Tirtov, and puts her gloved hand back to her tablet.

Tiffany's mention of Congress is all the Representative needs to take the floor. "Ms. Muth, I am wondering something. Did Mr.

Gabriel remind you of anyone?" I nod, because this Tirtov guy certainly reminds ME of someone.

"That's a ... weird question but ... yes," Allison says slowly. "He reminded me a little of a famous Gestalt psychologist who was the grandfather of a girl I dated in Connecticut. Gestalt therapists have a very aggressive style. I—"

"The point please?" I say.

"He wore horn-rimmed glasses like Gabriel's. And a big ring too. He was really cool about letting us sleep overnight, me and my girlfriend, in the same room in his postmodern glass house, and the next morning when I tried to make an omelet he stepped in and said, 'Let me take over, you're just tickling those eggs.'"

"And how did that omelet turn out?" asks the Representative.

"Best I ever ate," replies Allison. "In fact ..."

While Allison is explaining about the omelet, I think about my teaching supervisor. I'd like to show her Allison and the cowboy and the Representative. ALL these people take a lot longer to explain themselves than I do. They'd NEVER make it in the credential program.

The Representative nods at Allison and smiles warmly at her. "You know—I had a buddy in Afghanistan who had a traumatic battle experience and kept on confusing me with his brother. He loved his brother very much."

I'm not following where the Representative is going, but Allison is there before anyone else. "Are you saying I confused the psychologist with Mr. Tirtov and I turned them both into Gabriel?" Allison asks, clearly exasperated.

But the Representative is reassuring. "No, I don't think Mr. Tirtov's appearance is what they call a coincidence. I'm guessing that in your ... confused state, you might have imagined the psychologist guiding your way onto the train and providing you comfort. A kind of spirit guide."

"Like Virgil?" Allison says, and I have to say I'm impressed by anybody under 25 who knows enough to toss a Dante's *Inferno* reference into the conversation.

"Yes!" says the Representative, clearly knowing who she's talking about. "Believe me, I've seen cases like this; when a situation calls for assistance and none is present, a young and ... creative mind can imagine both the assistance and a trusted figure offering that assistance, even one that is not actually present at the time."

Allison looks up at the Representative, nodding slowly and somewhat sadly in agreement, and there's something in her large green trusting eyes that makes me want to argue with the guy. "So, you're saying Allison just imagined this old dude out of thin air? That's quite a hypothesis!"

But the Representative's patience with the voting public appears to be limitless. He continues to address Allison. "I cannot tell you what happened exactly. I can only describe what is possible, and quite normal for ordinary people under unusual stress. Just look at the facts. The man you imagined as Mr. Gabriel was himself a psychologist, remember? The real psychologist in Connecticut and the imagined psychologist Mr. Gabriel, one provided you with food and the other with drink. And when I ask you who does Mr. Gabriel remind you of? It all fits too well to be mere coincidence."

The Representative turns to me. "Perhaps as you suggest, Allison did not imagine Mr. Gabriel out of—how did you put it?—thin air. Perhaps she was accompanied on the train by someone she ... conflated with the psychologist in Connecticut. If not Mr. Tirtov here, then it could have been just about anyone else ... even you."

That's potentially rather flattering, don't you think? comments Inner Mack.

"Maybe you did conflate me with Gabriel," I say to Allison. "After all, you turned his scarf into a genuine Royal Stewart Tartan, when it was probably just some sales item from Walmart."

"Believe me," says Allison. "I wouldn't conflate you with anybody reassuring."

Oh well, says Inner Mack. *Keep working the kindness angle.* So I let Allison's remark hang in the air a little, and check out the other passengers. Tiffany Tolliver is concentrating on yet another speech by the former President. The cowboy's wife and child gaze fixedly out the window, as though they were in another world altogether.

"Hello!" breaks in a bright female voice from out in the hallway. "May I speak to the famous cowboy, please?"

11

May-Bel interviews Jimmy Shoulders

Viewers, look who I've found on our train to Canada! An actual cowboy. Isn't it interesting that during our whole voyage through America, it is only at the end that we are encountering a personality of the American West! And we are in the American East.

Mr. Shoulders has agreed to do an interview with me with the help of my voice translation app, because my English is not perfect (yet).

Is now a good time for that, sir?

Perhaps later?

Then perhaps would you sing a song for us?

It would be wonderful if you would perform one of your cowboy songs in the Observation Car, and I will film the reactions of the audience as well as the song!

You will do that later for us? Wonderful.

(Thanks to my voice translation app for helping me ask these questions to the cowboy and understand his answers. He speaks with a cowboy tone, which is quite difficult to understand.)

12

Mack tries to handle an increasingly bizarre situation

"Wait a second," I say. "Who are you exactly?"

We are now mostly alone back at a table in the bar of the observation car: me, Allison, and the young Chinese woman we met in Jimmy Shoulders' compartment. She is slender, petite, and wearing a wireless microphone with a small furry cover on top to block out wind noise. She has set up a second wireless microphone and small camera on the table. The camera flashes red, the microphone on the table flashes blue. If there's a flashing blue light on the mic the young Chinese woman is wearing, it's hidden under the bangs of that muff. Across the bar, the Black woman with the braids ignores us as she types on her MacBook.

The Chinese woman extends her hand. "I am Zhang Mei," she answers slowly in a voice that sounds a bit British, and a bit rehearsed. "But my American name is May-Bel. I am a student at Chongqing University travelling the U.S., and also a vlogger. You are part of the group that uses the pipes?"

Kind of cute, says Inner Mack. *But check out her wedding ring.*

"We're in the middle of a mystery," I tell her, after I tell her our names.

"Ah," she says. "Trains are so often myster-ious. I love the novels of Agatha Christie. I can read them all in Chinese. Also ... Raymond Chandler and James M. Cain. Perhaps I can help, and perhaps you can help me ... solve ... the mystery of my missing seat!"

Allison gets very excited. "You're from China? Chinese TV mysteries are the best! Do you know *Sleuths of the Ming Dynasty*? It's so good!"

May-Bel repeats the word "sleuths" into her phone. She smiles nervously. "Oh yes. It's a very good television drama, but long—with many episodes. And actors from Taiwan. I have never seen it, actually." She looks around, changes the subject. "What is the mystery we must solve?"

"We're trying to locate a missing friend of Allison's," I tell her.

"Who is your friend?" May-Bel asks.

"Gabriel," says Allison. "He's an older man. He's very nice. He ... helped me on the train. Now he has disappeared."

"The trouble is," I explain to May-Bel, "no one except Allison has seen him, so we're wondering if Allison imagined him."

"Imagined? Do you mean he is not a long time friend?" May-Bel asks.

"I met him for the first time today, and we talked for just for a little while," Allison replies. "Still he feels like an important friend, and I do not want to lose him."

May-Bel looks at Allison kindly. "You think, then, you did not imagine him?"

"I'm not sure what to believe anymore. Do you know what it is like, when you think one thing and everyone thinks something else?"

May-Bel nods. "Sometimes," she says carefully, "everyone is right."

I wonder if it's ok in China to think that that you are right and everyone else might be wrong. *Don't you always think that?* Inner Mack asks me. I wish I knew more about China.

"You've read Agatha Christie, right?" Allison asks May-Bel. "So, tell me: if this was an Agatha Christie novel, the case of the missing Gabriel, what would Hercule Poirot do to solve the mystery?"

May-Bel starts giggling. "What did you say? Huhhhr-quewl-pwah-hh-rohhhh." She can barely get the words out, she is laughing so hard. "Is that how you pronounce it in the United States?" I think Allison will take offense; after all, Allison's French sounds pretty good to me. But instead, Allison puffs out her cheeks and turns her palms to the air.

"Herrrrr-kewlll, Herrr-kewlll," she repeats, exaggerating her Fran-cais like she's in a bad Inspector Clouseau movie. And soon we're all doing this together, a crazy not-goth girl and a wannabe Salvadorian bagpiper bonding hysterically with a Chinese tourist vlogger over how badly we can mangle a French accent. "Herrrrr-kewlll, Herrr-kewlll." Only in America.

"Is this a private game?" asks the beautiful Black woman with the braids. "Or can anyone play?"

She is standing behind me—I did not see her cross the room. I stand up. I don't know what to say.

"We were," I stammer. "Me, Allison, May-Bel ..."

"Diamond," she replies. "Diamond Williams."

"Diamond!" May-Bel exclaims. "Like the stone."

But Diamond is way ahead of us. "Je suis heureuse de faire votre reconnaissance, May-Bel." And her French is so perfect, I'm afraid May-Bel will laugh. But she does not.

"Oh Ms. Diamond, that sounds so beautiful. What does that mean?"

Diamond smiles. "It means, I am pleased to meet you." She looks at me and Allison. A moment passes.

"We were just being stupid with French," Allison says. "But your French is perfect."

Diamond seems very distant. "No, it's I who should be sorry," she says to us. "My love of French got away from me. We poets get carried away easily. I guess I don't know how to play your game."

It's May-Bel's turn to break the uncomfortable silence. "Poet Diamond, I have a travel vlog on YouTube and also Chinese platforms, and my viewers would be so happy if I could interview you. Could I do that please?"

"I'm not sure ..." Diamond starts. Then she stops, looks to her right towards the door of the observation car. No one is there. She smiles out of one corner of her mouth and shrugs. "Sure," she says finally. "Why the hell not."

Diamond cocks her head to one side, towards the table where she was sitting earlier, then heads to the bar for a drink. May-Bel excitedly packs her camera stuff into a bag embroidered with bright flowers and fall leaves, and stands up to join Diamond. Then she turns to Allison and gives her a literal thumbs up.

"Interviewing many people," she says in her most carefully measured English, "is what Hercule Poirot would do to solve the mystery." And she heads off to join Diamond at her table.

"See?" I say to Allison. "You got to use an INDIRECT approach with people, not yell at them."

"But I really like yelling."

"Yeah, me too."

13

Mack learns secrets from surprising sources

"Remind me to NEVER do acid again," Allison says to me, after she's sure May-Bel is out of earshot. She's got that blue-ish tinge to her face. God, I hope she isn't coming down with something.

"So, now you think you may have imagined him?" I say.

"I don't buy the stuff about Afghanistan and projection," she says slowly. "But I guess somehow I made Gabriel up. Where did I get the name from? Something at Hebrew school maybe. Gabriel is one of the four protecting angels."

"You're Jewish?" I ask.

"Mostly," she says. "My parents aren't religious. But I had a *bat mitzvah* and I'm interested in metaphysical questions."

"I wasn't raised anything," I say.

"That means you're nominally Christian," she replies. "Like most people in the U.S."

I can hear Allison thinking *I feel sad.* I think that's what I hear. I almost say, "I feel sad too," when I remember something that happened right after my dad died.

"Mack," my sister said after the funeral. "Don't be sad for me. Let me have my own sadness. Give me the room to feel my own feelings."

For my class *Film Adaptations of Literature of the Absurd*, I wrote a paper where I argued that this is actually the problem with Meursault, the hero of *The Stranger* by Camus. Meursault isn't given room to feel any of his own emotions and so he kills someone and doesn't care. But it's hard to tell a visual story of someone with no room to feel. This is why there's never been a good film version of *The Stranger*. Unless you consider *Five Easy Pieces* an adaptation. Admittedly, a bit of a stretch.

I want to do that for my sister. Give her room to feel. And Allison, too. I want them to have the space to feel.

How can I help?

Food!

"It has got to be lunch time," I say. "Let's go to the dining car and get something to eat."

"Cool!" says Allison. "I haven't eaten in hours!" She excuses herself to go to the bathroom and I'm busy rocking back and forth on my heels when Diamond comes over. And gestures me to the back of the observation car, in front of a glass door marked "CAUTION." Beyond that door is a small balcony where two of my fellow bagpipers are smoking cigarettes, and beyond that, a view of railroad track receding from us.

"Listen," she says. "I do not want to upset your friend ... Allison. She seems a little distraught, a little all over the place." She looks me up and down. "And you just look ... a bit odd. But I feel like I can trust you. Can I?"

I nod, and then she lowers the boom.

"People on this train are lying to you."

She says it so matter of factly, I am not even tempted to argue. Her voice is steady and determined. I think of Representative Joe, and the easy way he has of saying things I don't believe. I wonder if I sound believable, when I go off on my intellectual tangents and lose the—

Focus! says Inner Mack, clearly annoyed. So I ask Diamond, "You mean, you've seen Gabriel?"

"I mean, people are lying to you and your friend."

"Who is lying?" I ask. "How do you know this?"

"I just know."

Diamond closes her eyes. Sighs. I ask myself, why are all the women in my life smarter than I am? Even the ones I've just met? I know Diamond will think more of me if I just nod wisely and keep my mouth shut. But that's a hard thing to do. Impossible in this instance.

"How do you know?" I ask again.

"I'll say this much. The guy I'm with—the Professor—he's lying about what he saw. About never seeing Allison before she confronted us in the observation car, asking about the old man. He saw Allison before that, when we were coming out of the bathroom. Just like Allison said. I saw her too."

"Wow," I say. Then I shut up because she isn't finished.

Diamond speaks rapidly, as though each word hurts her mouth and she wants to just get the pain over with as fast as possible. "If Russell is lying about the business in the bathroom, he could be lying about other things." She pauses and takes a deep breath. "Right? That's how it is with liars."

"Thanks," I say, but Diamond has already turned and walked away.

14

Diamond raises a rhetorical question

I walked out to the space between the observation and dining cars to clear my head, and now I'm back in the same damn bathroom again having an argument with Russell. Or rather I would if I could get a word in edgewise.

"You're back?" he says. "Well—"

Speech 1

"I'm telling you what I'm always telling you. You have to be careful. This writing world we inhabit. This delicate architecture where art talks to capitalism and capitalism capitulates but only while the spectacle captivates, while our small piece of the world—that still reads and thinks and is interested in such things—lingers fascinated over our gift for quirky, new and strange words. This architecture that we inhabit—a gallery if you will, a library, a refuge or sometimes it's only a pop up caravan—that architecture I keep on telling you Diamond, is FRAGILE. It can only take so much before the wheels come off the little airstream and the toilet stops working and you have to come to a halt on the freeway or wherever it is you're driving, and you have to flag down the cops and no one wants that. I know I'm being obscure. It's just that I keep on telling you we are very lucky and yes, *you* are lucky to be in this position and we have to be careful, and sometimes this little spot in the panopticon (that's a Foucault reference [yes, I know you know; I'm just reminding you]) is going to feel a bit cramped and over-surveilled, but we get to make art and have people look at it or at least pretend to look at it, and I don't know what else you can ask for. Yes, I know I have white male privilege. Diamond, I KNOW all that. You aren't telling me anything new here."

Speech #2

"Yes, I should divorce Marie; you'd like that, and I'd like that, except my kids wouldn't like it and my bank account wouldn't like it. It's expensive to get divorced. And I don't want to be poor again. I've been broke, lady, and it really isn't fun. There's no heroism in it, I don't care what anybody says.

"I wasn't going to tell you about the no-divorce until after the conference, because I wanted us to have this party. You know there's an actual dance party at the end of the convention, with a pretty good DJ and we can dance and enjoy and I have a nice hotel room that I got at a discount because the manager used to be a student of mine. He's actually a pretty good poet, and I thought this would be a beautiful weekend.

"So—let's *have* that weekend. I mean it's a fucking suite and there's champagne and we've got a couple's massage in the room scheduled and it will be—well it would be—grand.

"And there's our work. You always have such good ideas. Your insights are spot on, and your edits—that's why my last book got all those nominations. I know it, Diamond.

"You're old enough to know by now that there can be a moment that is so beautiful that you never forget it. We've had several. We can have more.

"You don't think I care about you but I do. You have meant everything to me—well not everything—but let's just say a hell of a lot, *and of course I'll help you*. I think you're brilliant. I just wish you'd be a bit more flexible, willing to roll with the punches. I KNOW that as a Black woman, you feel you have to fight every battle.

"But do you really have to fight all the damned time?

"Of course I love you. Of course I'll write your recommendations. Of course, I'll try to get that collection a publisher.

"But I'm not going to get involved with that stupid girl. Talk about white privilege! The quasi-Latinx-looking guy in the kilt? Please. So not worth our time.

"And what if it turns out to be a police matter? Remember that time you almost got arrested standing on the street smoking a cigarette?

"You're beautiful and I don't deserve you but maybe I deserve you a little because I'm the one who recommended that you come here in the first place on the fellowship that I helped you get."

"What do you want, a medal?" I say to him.

He closes his eyes, and—believe it or not—laughs.

"My mother always used to say that! She'd say, 'So you got that A in Latin, what do you want, a medal? Latin was the language spoken by Romans who destroyed our country and gave the Turks the idea to become an empire, and together they made it impossible for us to have a country, and by the time we got it into our heads to get it back they killed us and now we don't belong anywhere. We're truly stateless.'"

Russell keeps talking about art and transgression, but I have stopped paying attention. I'm thinking about secrets. How I don't like them.

I may not like secrets, but I've just created one that's actually a betrayal: I have dropped a dime on my lover and mentor. Will one secret more or less make a difference?

15

Mack discusses metaphysics and the origin of inequality while trying to eat lunch

We walk into the dining car. There are now flowers in vases on top of the white tablecloths, and a lot of well-dressed diners moving the flowers out of the way to make room for their cell phones. I do likewise. The Representative is sitting by himself, reading a newspaper. He does not look up as we pass him by, and I am grateful.

Allison sits down and we get a menu with what looks like a full course meal. Do I tell her now what Diamond told me? Not that Diamond said that much. "People are lying" doesn't mean that the supposed Gabriel is on this train.

I am trying to figure out what to say when the waiter brings us this fancy cold pink soup. Ok, I admit it. It's beautiful, this train. It looks like the photos the Vintage Trains Company posts on Instagram. I'm not into elegance as a general rule. But I can see why people like being in an old-timey space. It's a little like time travel.

Allison swings around the table, cell phone in hand, puts her cheek next to mine and takes a selfie that mostly features the pink soup. "Can I have a copy of that?" I ask, and she nods, taps her phone near mine to swap contact info, and texts me the photo. Miraculously the swap works, and I get the photo and the info. Normally I'm not one to document my lunch, but this move is a classic: ask for someone's phone photo, get their digits, and do it before you think you might even want them. Then call them later. "I just found your number on my cell phone, and I was wondering ..."

"I'm paying," says Allison, which is good news because—I don't have the jack for this kind of meal. Bad news is, I have no idea how or when to spill what I've learned from Diamond. If a woman offers to pay for your fancy train lunch, you don't reply, "Everyone on this train is lying to you, please pass the crème fraîche."

The best I can come up with is, "Then let me entertain you with my wit and charm." A lame suggestion, to which Allison responds by folding her hands under her chin and locking her eyes upon me in mock fascination. I know this is a cliché, but her eyes are green like the ocean is sometimes. You forget the dyed black hair and you just look at the eyes—they're pretty.

Another waiter comes by. "Drinks?" he asks.

"Hot chocolate for me," she says, and I say, "Yum that sounds good." Which I immediately regret. I should be getting something sophisticated like scotch, but the truth is I really want hot chocolate. It's a kid's drink. More innocent times. When the drink arrives it's an impressively huge steaming cup complete with a whipped cream peak.

This is really good hot chocolate. We look at each other, grinning at the treat.

Maybe I can slip the part about how we're being lied to into casual conversation, like when Eva Marie Saint informs Cary Grant he's wanted for murder while they're eating dinner on the train in *North by Northwest*. But for some reason all I can think about are the various iterations of *David Copperfield,* each of which begins with David's annoying self-introduction: "Whether I shall turn out to be the hero of my own life, or whether that station will be held by anybody else, these pages must show." God, what a bore. But people seem to like it so ...

"If I am to be the hero of my own life," I narrate to Allison, "I should point out that it's no exaggeration to say that Mackinnon Macdonald Flores' father left him with an appreciation for train travel as an alternate mode of transportation because he—Flores Sr.—loved Turner Classic Movies, and in particular movies about trains, and thus he bequeathed to Mackinnon a particular appreciation for narratives involving what Emile Zola called 'the infernal machine.'"

"*Chocolat chaud pissenlit de Japon,*" she murmurs.

"What?" I say.

"That's the imported Japanese hot chocolate Gabriel drinks."

"Jesus, Allison—I thought we were done with this."

"Gabriel made it himself, from this mix he likes and hot water from a coffee station, because the café wasn't open yet. I remember now. And the red plaid scarf he showed me." She smiles thoughtfully. "Cozy."

"Allison," I say again. "Can we let it rest long enough to enjoy lunch?"

"Sorry," she says. "Tell me about your parents. Did your dad play bagpipes too?"

The waiter comes with the rolls and I grab two because I'm hungry and she's paying.

"He did," I say with some reluctance, because I was kind of hoping to show off my knowledge of film history involving trains to demonstrate that I am actually a pretty deep and eccentrically interesting guy. "See, we're part Scot, so I couldn't help but inherit his love of music."

"Why couldn't you help inheriting that?" she says, taking the roll and shredding it into pieces.

"Because he didn't leave me anything else."

I expect her to say what they all say—like *I'm sorry for your loss* or even *that's a bummer.*

But the waiter comes by again. "For your *plat,* do you prefer calamari or lasagna *aux champignons*?"

"NO calamari!!!!" shouts Allison. "Can't you read my t-shirt?"

"*Excusez-moi,*" says the waiter abjectly. "*Lasagna pour deux personnes.*"

I'm about to ask her what's with her and this reverence for squid, but she barrels ahead. "Inheritances are tricky, aren't they? Few of us have any money, and few of us will get any from our families—the waiters, what do you think they earn?"

I'm about to answer when she leans forward and says: "I mean—do you even have a job? How many degrees do you have anyway?"

I take a deep breath and admit that in addition to the credential, I actually got a master's degree in Comparative Literature before doing the master's degree that I almost got in Film Studies. I thought—briefly—about working for a government agency or the Foreign Service. But I could never get an interview.

"See?" she says. "There are no jobs, and our government and everything—the way we live, the way we treat each other—it's fucked. I mean, we really need UBI and that's just for starters."

This is surprising, coming from a—I suspect—rich girl on acid singing "My Way" at the train station.

"True," I say cautiously. "My sister doesn't have a job. I don't know if I can get one. This teaching thing, I don't know if it will work out."

"That's why believing in something other than what you do for jobs is important," she says all of a sudden. "In Narrow Interior a bunch of us discovered that there was a secret religion that was practiced there. The Dankers. That's what they called themselves. The religion is a mixture of things, some Christian, some Shinto, some Buddhism, and there's even a touch of Judaism and Islam in there too, and when we put on our puppet play last year—the Dankers used puppets in their ritual performances—well, I thought for a minute I saw God."

How did we get from money to puppets and God? asks Inner Mack, and I'm thinking I can't very well interject what Diamond said about how we're being lied to, now that we're talking about such spiritual stuff. And I'm also thinking Allison probably really needs a decent meal after the whole ordeal with losing Gabriel, whether he be real or imagined.

"Where *is* God, do you think?" Allison interrupts my train of self-indulgent thought by actually tapping my hand with her soup spoon, while she leans over the table so far she threatens to knock over her own soup bowl and her hot chocolate cup.

I have absolutely no idea what to say.

I eat my roll and think. Stories that take place in trains don't usually feature discussions about God. On the train one talks about sex and spying and money. And death too, of course. One talks about divinity on a fictional journey, sure, but that's a quest where you might even run into an actual deity. Like in *The Journey to the West*, which is an olden days Chinese picaresque novel kind of like *the Wizard of Oz* featuring Buddhist manuscripts and talking animals. Or *Gilgamesh* where the title character is looking for the source for immortality, gets it, falls asleep and loses it. Or Paul seeing Jesus on the road to Damascus. Then again, most people are travelling on foot in the stories where these things happen. Not on a fancy train with white tablecloths and pink soup.

Wait. In my Berlin in Literature and Film class we saw *Wings of Desire*, and in that movie there's a moment in the subway where a woman prays and others meditate, and finally the Bruno Ganz angel character comforts a despairing man, who suddenly feels better.

Wenders. Always the rule breaker. But even Wenders took time off from rule-breaking to have lunch.

"I don't know if God is an entity that physically shows up places," I say at last. "But it doesn't change whether or not we do the right thing, does it?"

Allison laughs, then digs her spoon into the soup and slurps. "You're an idealist!" she says. "Mackinnon Macdonald Flores is a little idealist."

I've long ago scarfed up the soup. Now I look around wishing more food would come.

"I just think—you have to do what's right. I think that matters."

"To whom?" she says.

"It matters to me," I say. "And it matters to you and it ... makes things ... better."

"Go on," she says.

"Well, when you think the old guy exists you want to find him, because you are concerned about him. Rousseau says—"

"You mean Jean Jacques?"

"Yes."

"The *Origin of Inequality*?"

"Let me finish! Rousseau says that the one thing that redeems our fall into culture from our natural state is our empathy, our ability to feel pity for others. It's the one thing. You feel something for him—Gabriel—and you want to help. That's a good thing. Perhaps it's the only thing."

The lasagna arrives.

I look at Allison listening to me. I keep thinking she will laugh but she doesn't. She nods slightly as I talk. The sun is showing the roots of her hair, which aren't black, they're actually blue-blonde, almost platinum.

"Do you like me?" I ask her.

"You're ok," she answers. "Your teeth are kind of scarily white."

"Oh," I say. I eat my second roll. Grab my fork and start eating the lasagna.

Another waiter comes by with a garbage can, sweeping food bits off the table with a little brush and putting them in the trash.

"Madame," he says, smiling at her in this kind of phony dazzling way, "do you have any trash for recycling?"

She looks into the bin.

"It's the hot chocolate can!!!" she says.

"What?"

But the waiter has already gone off towards the kitchen. Swiftly, I might add.

"*Attendez*!" she calls after the waiter as she stands up. "It's the can of hot chocolate Gabriel used!"

"Take it easy Allison," I say, but it's too late.

She jumps onto our table, knocking over the lasagna and sending the breadbasket flying.

"Hey everyone, I know this is going to sound weird, but someone has disappeared from the train and we need to stop the train and alert the authorities and I need your support and cooperation."

She jumps from the table as the Representative rushes up and reaches for her arm.

"Ms. Muth, no. This is going too far." I grab her other elbow, but she wrenches her arms away and runs towards the kitchen, nearly knocking the legs out from under the waiter, who has returned with plates steaming with Cephalopoda. I run after her and hear the following exchange:

Waiter: "Oh Madame, I'm sorry I just put the garbage in the recycling bin."

Allison: "Let's go through it."

Waiter: "It's sealed up with all the garbage from the train."

She pushes him away, hard, then pivots and races towards the door of the observation car.

16

Mack fails at prevention

I try to catch Allison as she darts past me, and I manage instead to collide with the accountants who are carrying their leftover lunches as well as a fresh round of drinks, and now it is MY turn to knock them down. They fall with grace, managing to tumble, jump back up and not even spill their beverages. Then they continue walking, nattering away about merchandising and the cost of business travel.

Up ahead near the door to the observation car, Allison has stopped and is looking at something.

"Wait," I shout.

Allison glances back at me, and man I've never seen a more ferocious look on any woman. Except for maybe Elizabeth when she walked out on me.

"You never say how you feel," Elizabeth shouted. "You never WANT anything real. You just try to continually control your environment. As though you were 300 and not 30."

Well, she didn't say it. She thought it. At least, I thought she did. What she really said was, "You ignore me. Or when you don't, you just criticize everything. Like SAND in your butt crack."

Allison doesn't shout at me. She turns. Above her head is a glass box framed in red steel. A sign is painted on the glass in red letters: EMERGENCY BRAKE. Next to the box is a small hammer held to the wall by a chain and red metal clip.

This was in one of Dad's movies.

She grabs the hammer, breaks the glass, grabs the wooden handle hanging by a rope inside the box, and pulls hard. I brace myself. In the movies this is always a gut-wrenching moment with an ear-piercing screech, and I don't want to fall over and hurt anyone. The Representative grabs the table next to him as we ...

Keep right on going.

Either the emergency brake is there just for show, or it stopped working years ago and no one bothered to fix it. And it occurs to me that of course it's insane to have a working emergency brake in every car on every train because—to quote my dad—any Tom, Dick or Harry could pull it. You might just as well add a button on every 737 marked "push here to crash plane."

Allison stands there looking stunned and holding the emergency brake handle above her head like a strap on the city bus. In her other hand is the little red mallet she used to break the glass, which has come loose from its chain. She looks down at the hammer, then with chagrin at the other diners. Who have ... resumed their meals as if nothing in particular has happened.

If this were a movie, I guess this is where Allison would faint, so we could cut to the next scene where we're all having a drink or playing cards or doing the sort of thing people do casually on a train. Allison doesn't faint. She's ... I swear ... if she were from San Dimas, California,

I'd swear these are Serene Awareness™ cleansing breaths. One. Two. Three. She carefully places the hammer in the messenger bag she's carrying off one shoulder. Then with all the dignity a small not-goth rich girl can muster, Allison crosses the room, steps over our two overturned plates of lasagna, and resumes her seat across from me.

"Shall we order dessert?" she asks, with the frozen grace of Eliza Doolittle at an embassy ball. (That's Eliza played by Wendy Hiller, not Audrey Hepburn.)

"Dessert is on me," says a smooth voice from behind me. I turn. It is the Representative.

17

Diamond practices a fiction writing technique

I walk out of the bathroom and sit down in the observation/bar car and order another overpriced drink. Russell's tab.

In the MFA program, we had to take one course outside of our specialty. So I took a fiction workshop with an author who grew her own vegetables on an island off the coast of Seattle. She wrote magical realism. She says the key to good storytelling is knowing how to eavesdrop.

I'm sitting close to two businessmen in cheap suits. I can hear one side of their conversation.

"Adrian, I can't believe that girl tried to stop the train. With a delay like that, we could miss the *Pentagon Quatro Quatro* vs *Thanatos Tranquille* match."

"Right. I know you've always wanted to meet those amazing Mexican *luchadores*. That's why I didn't want to take this slow train in the first place. Even if you do hate to fly, we could end up missing the pre-match meet and greet if this train gets delayed."

"No Adrian, it won't help for us to talk to that girl. She disdains wrestling, remember? It is therefore a matter of complete indifference to her whether we arrive in time for what could be our big break or if we end our careers fighting at county fairs—if that is, we don't get hopelessly tangled up with Homeland Security. I'd even give her our tickets to **La Défiance – Super-Extrême** if I thought it would help."

"Yes, it is unfair, but there's a problem. That annoying girl happens to be right. The old man with the horn-rimmed glasses. He was right there with her. I would have said something, but we can't afford to get involved. Your issues with immigration are almost as bad as mine."

"I don't know how someone just disappears on a moving train. It's not like with wrestling. In a match, you just have the arena turn out all the lights. Before you turn them back on, you just move the guy you want to hide under the ring. Then the lights come back on, you have the heel stomp and sell the sudden disappearance like it's a global conspiracy!"

"True. That remains a mystery."

I lean back and put on my sunglasses. So, the businessmen in the cheap suits are professional wrestlers. And there WAS an old man with what's her name—Allison. I sit and feel less and less safe on this train with my professor/lover who I'm having a huge fight with. I wish DanieLa was here.

18

Mack considers a new alliance

The Representative goes off to find a waiter to remove our overturned lasagna and bring us dessert menus. I hope he asks if they can also replace the dinner rolls Allison scattered to the four corners of the dining car. I'm still hungry.

Focus! says Inner Mack. *The Representative won't be gone long.* And I think about how the girl and guy in train movies are doomed until the perfect friend conveniently materializes to assist them. Jill Clayburgh and Gene Wilder would have died on the *Silver Streak* without Richard Pryor's help. Even the couple in Hitchcock's *Strangers on a Train* gets a key assist from the ingenue's younger sister (played by Hitchcock's daughter!) to keep the police at bay.

"Allison, do you think we can trust Man of the People, Congressman Joe?"

"To help us find Gabriel?" she asks. I nod. She smiles for a moment with that far-away look in her eyes. "Yes, I ..." Then her expression changes; some of her ferocity returns. "So you finally believe me that Gabriel is on this train?"

"He seems to be." She pauses, to give me room to explain how she's right and I have been totally wrong. I pause too, because my explanation will require the big reveal about what Diamond told me.

Representative Joe returns. Without menus or dinner rolls. "Dessert will be here in a minute, and the campaign is paying," he tells us. "You kids must be hungry."

I'm about to protest that I am no kid, I'm 30 years old with almost two degrees and a credential, but Allison gets the next word in.

"We have something to tell you," Allison says to the Representative. She pauses, and stares at me expectantly.

"Representative Joe," I begin, still feeling awkward that I don't know this guy's last name. "I appreciate how you know about past trauma and identity conflation because of your time in Afghanistan. And," I add helpfully, "thank you for your service." That has to be a good way to begin! I lean into the table, and drop my voice in a way to inspire his confidence. "The thing is ... to borrow a phrase, certain new facts have come to light—"

The Big Lebowski? Inner Mack interrupts. *Seriously?*

"—And I ... we ... are reasonably certain that the older man Allison described to you is on this train."

"He is," says the Representative flatly, in a tone that means "he probably isn't."

"Or, he was. As I said, certain facts have—"

"Tell him about the cocoa tin," Allison interrupts, impatiently.

"The tin from the cocoa you remember drinking with your Mr. Gabriel," the Representative replies, cutting off the cogent and compelling recap I'm sure is on the tip of my tongue. "You've seen it?"

"Yes!" Allison says. "It was in the trash, the recycling bin the waiter brought around earlier."

"But you don't have this tin in your possession?"

"Joe," I add, "The tin Allison saw had a label, '*Chocolat chaud pissenlit de Japon*.' The same brand she told us about earlier. She couldn't have just imagined that."

"And you saw this tin, too?" the Representative asks.

"No," I reply. "But get this. One of the passengers told me, people on this train are lying to us about Gabriel."

"WHAT!" exclaims Allison. "WHO?"

"Diamond. Just before lunch. While you were in the bathroom."

"Thanks a lot for NOT sharing that info! I can't believe—" Allison starts sputtering and—once again—turning a bit blue. The Representative intervenes before Allison can form her explosivity into colorful words. (He doesn't seem to notice the blueness of her face.)

"So, you believe your Mr. Gabriel is on this train, possibly abducted but certainly missing. All on the circumstantial evidence of a piece of trash and a judgmental comment by a stranger?"

"You don't believe us?" asks Allison. A bit of light seems to set behind her eyes.

"I didn't say that," is the Representative's reply. "But I hope you are wrong." He produces a thin tabloid newspaper from a jacket pocket, and partially unfolds it in front of Allison. "I bought this at the last train stop. Do you recognize this person?"

The unfolded paper shows a black-and-white photo of a man. White. Older. Wearing glasses. Allison squints at it.

"It's not a very good photo," Allison says, trying to make up her mind. Then she looks up.

"Gabriel."

"You're sure."

"Yes. I told you. There's something in his expression."

The Representative nods. "I was under the impression that you were looking for a *Mr.* Gabriel. It did not occur to me that Gabriel might be his first name." He points to the caption below the newspaper photo. "Mr. Gabriel Solomon. Quite a well-known man in this region."

Why didn't you think to pick up a newspaper? Inner Mack asks me. I fight back feelings of inadequacy.

"Just who is Gabriel?" I ask.

The Representative lowers his voice. "He's an advocate for the rights of migrants and refugees. What you might call, an activist. He works closely with a local organization led by undocumented immigrants, and he's become the enemy of many on the far right of our politics who cry 'America First' and seek to close our border with Mexico. And Canada."

He opens his tabloid newspaper to reveal the entire front page. The headline reads:

GABRIEL SOLOMON SOUGHT FOR IMMIGRATION
CRIMES
REWARD OFFERED FOR SOLOMON'S ARREST

I whistle softly. The Representative continues in a surprisingly dulcet tone for a politician. We have to huddle close to hear him.

"I told you earlier, I hope Mr. Solomon is not on this train. A train is a difficult place to hide, and of course once we reach the border, this train will be crawling with immigration officials. But if anyone knows how to avoid detection by Homeland Security, it would be your Mr. Solomon."

"Are you saying," asks Allison, "that Gabriel might be better off if we stopped looking for him?"

"My friend," the Representative replies, "I'm saying that if you and ..." he gestures to me as if I am nameless, "blunder around this train like a modern-day Nancy Drew and Ned Nickerson, you may put Mr. Solomon in grave danger."

(Ted Nickerson, I think unhelpfully. In the 1930's *Nancy Drew* film series, the filmmakers changed the name of Nancy's co-detective from Ned to Ted, because they thought "Ned" was insufficiently masculine and the writers wanted to invoke Teddy Roosevelt.)

"Not that this would matter to someone like Solomon," Joe presses on. "He's not afraid of prison. But there are hundreds, perhaps thousands, of asylum seekers and undocumented migrants in this region who look to the work done by the likes of Mr. Solomon as a source of hope and inspiration."

I look at Allison. If her green eyes were big before, they are just about popping out of her eye sockets now.

"Woah," she says. "This is huge."

"So for God's sake," the Representative says, turning his attention from Allison (Nancy) to me (Ned/Ted), "please don't blurt out your suspicions to every person you meet on this train."

"But we just blurted them out to you!" Allison says.

The Representative smiles, lowering his voice even further.

"Luckily, I'm on your side. If Gabriel Solomon is on this train, I will help you try to find him, and ascertain that he is safe."

The Representative is interrupted by the waiter, this time rolling a dessert tray.

I can hear my mom telling 10-year-old me, "You can't make a meal out of dessert." But I'm about to try.

19

Mack receives a gift

I hit the men's room in the second-class car, then exit to stand outside for a moment between the second-class and dining cars. You can actually do that on this train. The cars are joined on right and left by a bellows-like divider to keep the heavy drinkers from falling out, but this divider doesn't fit right and a stiff breeze blows through its gaps. Brrr. I forgot this is the fucking Northeast and it's still cold here. My poor SoCal legs! But it's bracing too, and for a minute the petit fours (more than four) and eclairs I've just hoovered for dessert aren't weighing as heavily on me.

Another one of Dad's favorite movies was about a Hollywood director who decides he wants to find out what being poor is like, so he pretends to be a hobo and hops a freight train (with a gorgeous blonde in tow, of course), but he quickly catches a cold and sneezes his way through the first half of the film. But, unlike me, he wasn't wearing a kilt.

I can't afford to get sick on this trip. My health insurance is—shall we say—minimal.

I shiver and realize I should forget all about Allison, who right now is polishing off yet another hot chocolate while the Representative sips his wet double cappuccino. Some man of the people he turns out to be. But she seems to kind of like him—as much as she likes anybody—and the last thing I want to do is get involved in some *Jules et Jim* situation. Two men and one girl is not my idea of romance, not that I'm romantically interested in Allison.

Fucking *auteur* theory. So are we meant to think about film as some kind of collective creation? If so, what do we do with ...

To my right, some member of the janitorial staff appears and starts rooting through items in a trash bag. He drops some things into a smaller blue container and (when he thinks no one is looking) has the nerve to just toss some stuff out the train through a gap in the bellows divider. Recycling, I guess he calls it. And I'm thinking I really should just focus on getting on with my pipe band conference and finishing my credential, when to my right something colorful flaps by in that horrible freezing northeast wind.

It's a scarf. Momentarily caught in a gap in the divider between the train cars. I reach for it over the head of the janitor. I catch it.

Well fuck me. This scarf is Royal Stewart tartan. "Hey," I yell to the janitor, "why did you throw that out?"

"*Ce n'est pas moi,*" he answers back. And he could be right. It could have come from somewhere towards the front of the train. The janitor looks at my kilt. "*C'etait a vous?*"

I have an idea.

"The garbage," I say. He looks quizzical, so I just grab the trash bag he's holding. He lets me look through it. Not a fun experience, but ... about halfway down, a metal can reads, "*Dandelion hot choco- late—product of Japan.*"

"*Assez*," he says. And grabs the cocoa can as the *maître d'* comes back.

"Can I help you, sir?"

"Uh no," I say. "Just chatting." The janitor looks at the maître d', who nods. The janitor then tosses the can out of the train.

"The environment, you guys!" I say. They shrug their shoulders and go back to work.

Inner Mack is super excited. *Royal Stewart tartan, dude. Gabriel's scarf.* I take another look at the scarf. Surprise! It's a really nice tartan weave. Not hundreds of dollars' worth of nice, like my kilt. But, nice. If I were Allison and someone offered to lend me this scarf, I'd mosdef say yes.

Strange. But Allison's affection for this scarf is another point in her favor. I stuff the scarf in the sporran attached to my kilt and walk back to the table with Allison and the Representative.

"How long does it take for you to use the damned bathroom?" Allison demands. "Gabriel could be dead by now." Her hot chocolate is drained. I don't dare look at my watch. I couldn't have been gone all that long.

"What's our next move?" the Representative asks me.

The Rep seems to be getting with the program at last, Inner Mack observes encouragingly, *and the fact that he hasn't mentioned acting, Afghanistan or med school is a good sign.* I nod to my inner self. My thoughts turn to the scarf that just flew into my grasp from the front of the train somewhere. That's the direction to head.

"Let's take another look in first class," I tell them.

20

May-Bel learns about professional wrestling

Hello dear Viewers! Here I am having a snack in the Observation Car with my new friends Sayid and Adrian.

First let me say something about my snack which is something called "a pig in a blanket." This is a hot dog pastry, like ones you find in bakeries in China, only Americans serve these pastries extremely hot, not at room temperature like we do. I burned my mouth taking the first bite! But strange to say, I like hot pigs in blankets. Americans eat them with a mild mustard. Thumbs up! Also I am drinking a Coke, which I think is sweeter than what we drink in China. It is too sweet for me.

But now let me introduce to you my new friends.

I have just learned something fascinating about my train companions. They are professional wrestlers. If you live in Shanghai you may have seen professional wrestling in the WWE, the World Wrestling Entertainment. But I have never seen this, and I have many questions.

Sayid and Adrian together: Hello out there, viewers of May-Bel's vlog!

May-Bel: Hello viewers! Here are Sayid and Adrian and as you can see—

Adrian: I'm much better looking than Sayid.

Sayid: Yet somehow, the girls like me best.

Adrian: Better hope your wife isn't listening, mate!

May-Bel: (laughing) You are both very handsome! But you are not very ...

Sayid: Buff?

Adrian: Hunky? Like The Rock? Ah. Wrestlers today are often smaller than in the past. So we can move faster, be more athletic.

Sayid: We might look more hunky out of these suits.

May-Bel: Please explain your profession to us. I read on the Internet that professional wrestling is pretend fighting.

Adrian: Don't think about it in terms of pretend or real. The physical interactions we engage in are real. But we do play characters, as in a drama.

May-Bel: So this is a performance? Like a fight in a movie?

Sayid: It's like a movie, in that we are performing in character.

Adrian: But not like a movie. Because we're really doing many of the things you see us do. So, watch. I will pull up my shirt and Sayid will really hit me. Go ahead, Sayid.

SLAAAAAP!

May-Bel: Ouch! I could feel that! How does that not hurt?

Adrian: It DOES hurt. But you get used to it. Kind of!

Sayid: I hit Adrian hard. Look at that red welt on his chest. But with an open hand in a way that would spread the impact and not injure him. Don't break the skin, don't break a bone. We have to finish the performance. And perform again the next night and the night after that.

Adrian: People in our business do get hurt sometimes, because—like I said—the physical things we do are real. But we do our best not to hurt each other. In this sense all combatants are helping each other do the stunts we do.

May-Bel: Can you show us more?

Sayid: Sure. Let's try something more elaborate. This is called a piledriver. What Adrian is going to do is drive my head into the floor. Watch. We stand and face each other. Now, Adrian is going to kick me in the stomach, and I'm going to double over with my head between his legs. OOOF!

Adrian: I hit Sayid hard, but not hard enough to hurt him. He has to sell the kick, by making a noise, and maybe spitting a wad of gum across the room, so you believe he's really suffering. But I kicked him, just to have him bend over in front of me, ready for the next move. I'm going to make something called an S-Lock with my hands, and then Sayid is going to put his hands around the back of my thighs and squeeze my legs against the sides of his head to protect his neck.

Sayid: I don't know if you can hear me from this position. I need to get my legs up so that I'm as straight as possible.

Adrian: And now I will grab Sayid's waist and just sit down right here in the aisle between the chairs and tables.

CRAAAAASH!

May-Bel: Oh no! The whole car shook when you did that! Sayid, he is really hurt.

Sayid: No, no May-Bel. It just looks like I crashed my head against the floor.

Adrian: Mate, she looks a little ... green around the gills.

Sayid: I recommend you *don't* do your signature roar with your tongue hanging out.

Adrian: No ... maybe not.

May-Bel: Wait. I'm ok. I'm ... ok. So the show is and is not pretending. It ... let me breathe for a moment. Ah. What you do looks ... very frightening. But you are not hurt, Sayid.

Sayid: I'm fine. But that floor is a bit hard, so I'm glad Adrian sat down gently. Yes, there are accidents, and sometimes the move goes wrong. But the fact is we don't want to hurt anybody. Wrestling is about mimicking violence to avoid violence. Because we don't want to see anyone hurt or wounded or dead. We are here because we want to love everyone. We DO love everyone.

May-Bel: I ... don't ... understand.

Adrian: Our performances are all about generating emotion—that's the most important part of it.

Sayid: This is where our characters come in. We fight in character, not as ourselves. Adrian's character is, the king of the heels, a bad guy in wrestling terms. His name is *Le Salaud*, which is French for "bastard." But he's had many other names, because he keeps on switching promotions because he keeps on making political comments and is such a troublemaker!

May-Bel: A troublemaker really? Or pretend.

Sayid: Some of both!

Adrian: Even I don't know sometimes!

May-Bel: Then Sayid, you are the good guy?

Sayid: We call good guys "baby faces," or "faces" for short. I am a face who's good at suffering. I make you feel sorry for me when I take those hard chops. I lose a lot. Then at the end of the match when it seems I've been utterly defeated, I stand up, after staggering for quite a bit and limping. At the very end of the runway, I suddenly breathe and stand tall.

Adrian: He stands for everyone who has been beaten down. When he stands up, we all survive. We fight on. The dream lives. Even and especially after we lose.

Sayid: It's our job to thrill you with our moves in the ring, then tear at your heart with the drama we create. Anything you can see in a great movie, we create too. A friendship betrayed. A tyrant crushing the weak. A bully reigning supreme. But also, the arrogant humbled. Brains over brawn. Even comedy.

May-Bel: Do some of the people who come to see you ... want to see blood?

Sayid: Some. Not many. You're allowed to feel anything in and around what we're doing—it's ok—and we're helping get it out of our systems so we don't hurt anybody in real life.

Adrian: Afterwards we go home and whatever wickedness we had inside of us, whatever anger we had—we all leave it inside the corners of that ring, which is square, so there's room for things to get put and cornered and contained.

May-Bel: This is so interesting. But I need to ask. Adrian, you are a troublemaker? And Sayid, you too?

Sayid: More like, trouble finds me. I'm a resident of Canada, but I am originally from Syria. You know about the troubles there, May-Bel?

May-Bel: Yes. I do.

Sayid: As an Arab and a Muslim, I am not always regarded kindly by the U.S. government. Homeland Security.

Adrian: I'm a Brit but I have run a bit afoul of many wrestling promotions, because I am trying to form a wrestler's union.

May-Bel: Ah. Like the All-China Federation of Trade Unions. A worker's collective.

Adrian: Yes. Um ... yes. Our work is rewarding. But dangerous. We need the protections other workers take for granted, like health insurance and a pension for old age. So we can focus on doing what we love. Making our audience happy and excited.

Sayid: Would you come see us wrestle in Merveilleux City? Assuming we get over the border without incident.

May-Bel: I would love to see a wrestling show!

21

Mack makes sense of the baggage car

Allison and I move through the second- and first-class hallways. The Representative trails a bit behind, as if he's second-guessing his decision to help us. And as we proceed, I think about how this whole mess with Gabriel reminds me of a bunch of different stories. They all involve murder and mayhem on trains.

"Allison, doesn't this situation remind you of a book?"

"Not really. I don't read much."

"A movie then," I insist.

"Like *the American Friend?*"

"You mean the Wim Wenders movie? No. I'm thinking of something else."

She ponders. "You mean like *Trading Places*, where the bad guy ends up trapped in a gorilla suit in a cage in the baggage car?"

"God no. I'm thinking like one of the Hitchcock movies."

"For Christ's sake, Mack, that's not helpful. Don't they all take place on trains?"

I'm counting the number of Hitchcock movies with trains in them when we arrive in first class. "Let's say a quick hello to our friends in first," I suggest to Allison. She lifts her eyebrows and nods. We look to see what is happening with Tiffany, the Shoulders Family and Tirtov. But their compartment has the curtains drawn over the windows. Allison gingerly tries the door handle.

Locked.

I turn to the Representative. "Any idea how to get into a closed compartment?"

"You don't," he tells me. "People have a fundamental right to their privacy."

"We need to see what's going on in there!" Allison insists.

But the Representative is equally insistent. "You can't break down the door. You're going to have to find another way."

I'm about to argue when I notice Allison trying the glass door at the front end of the first-class car. This one is labelled EMPLOYEES ONLY. This must be the train's baggage car.

"*Trading Places*," Allison mutters.

"You can't go in—" begins the Representative. But Allison is already in.

I'm wondering how Tiffany Tolliver's compartment is locked and the baggage car is unlocked. An enterprising type might just waltz into baggage and equip themselves with enough bagpipes for a National Tartan Day parade. April 6th, in case you're curious.

The Representative looks nervously down the hallway. "I'm not going to tell you kids what to do," he tells me. "But I can't be involved in trespassing on a train."

"Well then, just stand there," I reply. "And if you see anyone coming, knock three times hard on the baggage car door." And before he can reply, I dart through the doors and join Allison in baggage.

The car is crammed with a tower of boxes labelled **Musée Danker, Merveilleux City**, suitcases of various sizes, and a bunch of crates filled with wine bottles. It's a mess in here. I'm glad I didn't check my bagpipes. There's even a big carpet that has come partially unrolled propped up against the wall. I mean, what are they doing? Redecorating?

Allison jabs me in the ribs and points. A particularly large crate covered with a cloth is moving. A vague sort of whining is coming out of it.

"Gabriel, we're here!" she cries. We both rush towards the crate. I pull the cloth off the top, and it's ...

Corgis. Five of them. In a large wire cage. On the front is a big printed label:

Best in Show winners 2021 All-American Dog Show
Emerson, Thoreau, Melville, Dickinson, and Alcott
Owned by Spencer Peabody

"ARFF!!!!!" exclaims one corgi. Thoreau, probably. He was the noisiest of the transcendentalists. The other four wag their tails and look at us. Probably hoping to be released from dog jail, or at least have a snack.

"Corgis are supposed to be the smartest dogs!" says Allison, reaching her fingers through the crate gaps to pet two other corgis. I bet they're Alcott and Dickinson. Female solidarity.

"Well, then why can't they tell us where Gabriel is?" I retort. I'm not a dog person—something else that Elizabeth didn't like about me.

"They probably *do* know! We just don't speak their language." One of them barks back at Allison, agreeing completely. We start moving the boxes and crates and seeing what else might be here.

I flip open a case. Glittery cloaks, and big leather belts encrusted with fake gems that spell out *Number 1 Tag Team Champions*. "Professional wrestling gear!" Allison says. "I haven't seen any hunky guys on the train. I wonder where they are."

"Stay focused," I say, as I keep rummaging. "Whatever we find, we have to do it soon, before we're discovered. Say ... do you think Gabriel might have a checked bag in this car?"

"I have no—"

"Think, Allison," I interrupt. "Did you see him with baggage? Maybe on the platform before you both got on the train?"

"Not luggage," she replies. "But I think I did see him on the platform ... with all these orthodox relatives seeing him off."

"Greek Orthodox?"

"Jewish Orthodox. They were wearing all black and white and looking a bit like the Mennonites."

"Who?"

"There are some of them in Narrow Interior. Some of them became Dankers."

I'm turning over cases and trunks as she tells me more about the Dankers, how they were originally a breakaway subgroup of Anabaptists from Germany, Switzerland and Japan.

She sure talks a lot. But it's pleasant.

I jab my elbow on something. It's a life-size cutout of the cowboy guy, Jimmy Shoulders. Leaning against the cutout is a tube. I open it up. It's one of those roll down signs like they have at conventions sometimes.

WELCOME TO THE EVANGELICAL
CHRISTIAN RODEO AND
MUSICAL REVIEW STARRING
JIMMY SHOULDERS
(real life descendent of Will Rogers)

Allison walks towards me and gives Shoulders the once-over. "Wasn't Will Rogers Native American?" she asks.

"How the hell do you know that?" I say.

"As a pretty much Jewish person, I'm interested in hybrid identities."

"Yeah, well I'm a little bit Latinx, and you don't see me carrying on about it."

"Say," she says. "Are you maybe a little bit Jewish?"

I roll my eyes. "That's a new one. Salvadorian yes, Jewish no."

"You never know," she says. "Have you done a DNA test?"

"I don't have the money for that."

Allison nods. "So what d'you think is the story with Jimmy Shoulders?" she asks.

We look at the acts featured on the poster:

Watch Jimmy Shoulders lasso
a sinner right from the audience!
Crack whips and make
money changers disappear!
Perform the famous Will Rogers
rope trick and sing his hit single
"Jesus Is My Kind of Cowboy"!

"I don't think he's the nice sort of Christian," Allison offers.

"How did he make Gabriel disappear?" I ask her.

"Shoulders didn't make him disappear," Allison says. "He doesn't have that kind of power." She turns blue again, just for a moment. "You can't always control disappearance. I had an octopus tattoo, but it disappeared somehow, and went inside of me."

I decide to ignore that particularly weird piece of information.

"When you get to Merveilleux City, you should get yourself checked out by an actual doctor," I tell her. "You kind of turn blue sometimes."

"It'ssssss not a problem," she says.

I turn away and examine an oversized suitcase. I pull it towards me just as the train lurches, knocking me backwards into Allison. We fall, together. I intuit something sibilant, but no words.

"Oof," she says. Because I've fallen on top of her.

I'm silent. Because I am suddenly feeling extremely comfortable.

For just a moment I feel at home, like we could turn on the TV or snooze, or we could talk about what books we are reading (well not reading in her case), or we could—

"Get off of me you big dope!" says Allison, somewhat muffled, because I've shifted and now she is actually speaking into my armpit.

"Oops," I say.

I roll off and sit next to her as I take inventory of the baggage car: five corgis, multiple suitcases, assorted bagpipe bags, the boxes for the Musée Danker, glittery costumes, the half unrolled carpet and the life size cutout of Jimmy Shoulders. If there's any sign here pointing to Gabriel, I'm not seeing it.

"*Alors*, police commissionnerrrrr," says Allison, reprising her fake French accent. "I—Inspectorrrrr Poirot—declarre this gentleman officially kidnapped."

"No," I say. "This isn't *The Lady Vanishes*."

"Is that the one where everybody is the murderer?"

"No, that's *Murder on the Orient Express*." Funny how girls seem to like that film.

"*De toute façon, je doute que Gabriel soit mort*," Allison says. "He's old but in very good health, from what I could see."

I say, "It happens like that sometimes, though. People seem fine one day and the next day, they're gone."

She sighs. "*Oui c'est vrai*—It's a terrible shock to everyone else, but dying suddenly is probably a better way to go than lingering and having people asking over and over if you're dead yet."

"This has gotten serious all of a sudden," I say.

"I do that," she says. "I go from playing with corgis and French accents to talking about death. It's hard for people."

I think for a moment. "It's ok," I say. And I mean it.

"But seriously, police commissionerrrr," she says. "Let's review the facts."

"Arf," says one of the corgis. I think it's Melville this time.

"We have an elderly gentleman named Gabriel who has disappeared, and everyone insists feverishly he was never here in the first place. *C'est correcte?*"

"*Oui.*" I say.

"We know I saw Gabriel. Diamond says we're being lied to. But why?"

"I have no idea," I say. "But I'm only the police commissioner and the cop is always something of a dolt."

"I will now astound you with my brilliance, Police Commissioner," Allison says in an imperious voice. "*Les autres,* they don't want to face an inquiry or any kind of investigation or get the cops involved."

"Maybe," I say, "but that still does not tell us where Gabriel is. The Representative is right on one thing: it's hard to hide someone on a train. Unless Gabriel is a contortionist and is in one of these trunks like the guy in *Ocean's 11* who left Cirque du Soleil to participate in the heist."

"I think that's *Ocean's 13.*"

"Whatever."

We sit and look around.

"That carpet is cool," Allison says. "I wonder why they just threw it in here like that."

"You know what, Commissaire," I say. "In this light, your eyes are not green; they're almost violet looking."

She shakes her head at me. "Stop trying to be gallant, it's stupid. You're confusing me with someone else. Elizabeth Taylor. She had violet eyes."

"She was in a lot of terrible movies," I say, trying to skip past how my flattery fell flat.

"Which one do you think was worst?"

We both jump to our feet.

"CLEOPATRA!"

"Where she shows up at Julius Caesar's bedroom," I say.

"Hidden in a rolled-up carpet!" she shouts, as we both rush to the carpet roll to unwrap it. Wouldn't it be amazing if Gabriel were tucked in there like Liz was? That would be an awesome plot point.

But nope. He's not in there.

We spread the carpet out. No Gabriel. But there is a big silver ring with an amber stone in it. Didn't Allison describe Gabriel earlier as wearing a large ring?

"He WAS here," Allison says. She looks at the inside of the ring and shows me the inscription. I read it out loud.

"*To S with love*"

"S for Solomon!" Allison exclaims. "So they attacked him, rolled him up in the carpet, unrolled him and now where the hell is he?"

"Allison, a ring with an 'S' inscribed in it doesn't prove anything."

"You're off-kilter," she replies.

"What?"

"Your kilt. It's gone ... off kilter."

I look down, and she's right, my kilt has yanked a bit sideways. Probably from when I fell on her. But before I can adjust it, she's there before me, kneeling down to give it a gentle twist into position. And I guess it's due to her being short to begin with and shorter when she kneels, because when she rises to her full height her smile is cockeyed.

"You're quite the dresser, Mackinnon Macdonald Flores," she tells me. "An outfit so completely thought out, there are plaid boxers underneath the plaid kilt."

I blush. "It could be worse," I tell her. "Lots of kilt wearers go commando."

"Bye Corgis!" Allison says. "I wish you could come with us!" They bark in reply as we leave the baggage car. Allison is right on the money. They really do seem to be very smart dogs.

22

The Kid

My real mom is pregnant. She and my real dad have not come here yet. Or my older brother. Too hard.

I am living with my aunt in Massachusetts. It was hard to get here. Many miles in the back of trucks and walking on foot. It cost a lot of money to leave. But it was not safe for me to stay in Nicaragua, my parents said.

It is not safe for them either. But there is not enough money now for all of us to leave. So, I am the first to go.

But now my aunt says, it's not safe for me to stay in Massachusetts, not without papers.

The janitor at our school says he knows someone who can help. Someone who can get me papers—real ones this time. And maybe, papers for my whole family. But I cannot stay in Massachusetts. I must keep moving north.

All I need to do is pretend. Take a ride on a train and pretend to be a son of a cowboy. I am the right age and the right type, he tells me, and I speak English well.

I am frightened. But I can do this. Like I did in the church play. I got to be a shepherd. I got to worship the baby Jesus.

"You just look at the stained glass window," my teacher told me.

Just look.

23

Mack receives some surprises

When we exit the baggage car and re-enter first class, the Representative is gone, but Shoulders is waiting for us. His "aw shucks" "howdy pard'ner" vibe is gone. Replaced by something colder, with narrowed eyes and veins bulging from his neck. He blocks our way.

"What the hell were you doing in the baggage car?" he asks me. Without a trace of an accent this time.

"Just checking things out," I tell him, trying to sound casual. "There's a nice cardboard figure of you back there, cowboy. Seemed a hell of a lot more cowboy than you do."

I do not see his punch before I feel it, and I do not feel the punch until after it floors me. It's a nice punch, I'm forced to admit, neatly clipping the point of my chin so I'd feel the impact of the sterling silver ring he'd slipped onto one knuckle for the occasion, and he'd feel very little at all. It's a punch that knows how to behave. It's been practiced before. At least that's what I think I'm thinking. I'm not thinking too clearly. I don't even remember exactly how I got from standing in front of Shoulders to sitting where I am, back against the door of the baggage car, holding my jaw.

OW! says Inner Mack. *You walked right into that!*

"You better not have messed with anything back there," Shoulders says, gesturing to the baggage car. Still threatening.

"We weren't the first ones there today," Allison replies defiantly. And she shows Shoulders Gabriel's ring.

"Where'd you find that?" Shoulders demands. "It's mine. I want it back."

"You know damn well it isn't yours," Allison replies. Unafraid. Of course she's unafraid. She wasn't the one Shoulders just punched out. And as Shoulders lurches one menacing hand towards Allison, a friendly face pops out of her compartment two doors down the first-class hallway.

"Long time no see," says May-Bel cheerily, waving us in to join her. Just that quickly, Shoulders reverts to the cowboy: friendly, trusting, face open like a prairie. The open hand he'd intended for Allison is now extended to me.

"Here Slim, let me help you up," he says to me, pulling me to my feet. "You gotta be careful in these old trains. They're none too steady going around a bend."

He disappears quickly into his compartment. We hear the compartment door lock behind him. Somewhat groggily, I follow Allison into May-Bel's compartment.

With the crowd ever-present around Jimmy Shoulders, I haven't had a chance to clearly see what one of these compartments looks like. First-class passengers sit on one of two facing benches upholstered in reds and browns like Victorian sitting room couches, only these couches have a center fold-down bolster where the Victorians could lay their knitting or cocaine or whatever they brought with them into the compartment. Above each couch are etched glass sconces, and above them black wire mesh shelves for luggage.

"I thought I heard a fight just now in the hallway," May-Bel says.

"You did," Allison replies. "Nothing serious. Just some testosterone fueled nonsense."

"Hey," I protest. "It wasn't any of *my* testosterone."

May-Bel sits in the corner of one couch by a large window divided horizontally. The top half of the window contains brass handles so it can be lowered to let in fresh air. I feel a breeze come from behind as Allison moves forward to examine the window. A cold, wet breeze.

"This has been a very interesting train ride so far," May-Bel tells us. "I am excited for the opportunity to interview such interesting people for my vlog."

"How did the interview go with Jimmy Shoulders?" I ask.

"We haven't had the interview yet. But don't worry! He's going to perform for us later. In the Observation Car!"

"That should be unforgettable," I say.

"What about Congressman Joe?" Allison asks. "Have you interviewed the Representative for the United States Congress?"

May-Bel is quiet for a moment, absorbing our words. "I tried. It was ... interesting."

Something is wrong, Inner Mack says.

"What did you talk about?"

"I do not know, exactly. He speaks very quickly. He said our talk would be off the record. What does that mean?"

"It means that you can report what you learned," replies Allison. "But you can't say you learned it from Joe."

"I did not know that," May-Bel says slowly. "I thought 'off the record' meant no recording. I turned off my equipment. Then he talked a lot. About money, I think."

"What did he say about money?" I ask.

"He talked about his next election," May-Bel says, pressing her lips together between each word. "About how he needs money to win the election, and how expensive it is. I had trouble understanding him."

"Sounds like you understood him just fine," I tell her, with a roll of my eyes.

"Oh, shut up," Allison says to me. Then to May-Bel: "I'm sure he was only trying to be friendly, and most Americans talk about money all the time, so that's no surprise. Remember, he's trying to help us find Gabriel."

May-Bel nods, but her lips remain tightly pressed.

"Did he say anything else?" I ask May-Bel.

"He talked—I think—about the relationship between the United States and China. How it is very bad right now. He asked if people in the United States have been friendly to me, or if I have heard unkind words."

"Has that happened to you?" Allison's eyes grow even larger, and watery.

"A few times, but I do not think about it," May-Bel says seriously. "When countries are friends with each other, the United States and China, that can change, and change again. Like the weather. But people? People from any place can be friends, and friendship should last forever."

"Is that what Joe said?" Allison asks.

"It is what *I* say," May-Bel replies. "Mr. Joe, he says he wants China and the United States to be friends. That we can help each other. He said he can help me too."

"But how could he help you?" I wonder. This is sounding like a weird conversation.

May-Bel's unhappy face returns. "He said he knows who my father is. How my father is a wealthy man who does business in the United States. How my father needs friends in the United States right now, more than ever. I wanted to ask Mr. Joe more questions, but then Mr. Shoulders came and asked to speak to Mr. Joe."

"I'm sorry you didn't have your camera on to record that conversation," Allison says. "We could help you figure it out."

I resist the urge to tell them what I think about the Rep and his friendliness.

"Thank you," May-Bel says. She smiles, and her lips relax, her face returns. "But I think first we should solve the mystery of Mr. Gabriel. Unless you found him already—yes?"

"No. Well, kind of," Allison starts. She tells May-Bel about our search in the baggage car, and shows May-Bel the ring.

"If Mr. Gabriel is no longer in the baggage car, then where can he be?" May-Bel asks.

"He could be in the compartment with Mr. Shoulders and his family," I tell her.

"I suspect that's where he is," pronounces Allison. "But the door is locked. They won't let us in."

"I have an idea," May-Bel says. She reaches into her camera bag, pulls out a selfie stick and extends it. It extends quite far.

"You think you can take a picture of their compartment from the outside?" Allison asks. May-Bel nods, and attaches her little camera to the end of the stick. She hands her cell phone to Allison.

"You can see what the camera sees using this app," May-Bel tells Allison. "Just hit the red button at the bottom of the screen when you want to take a picture." May-Bel lowers the top half of her compartment window and sticks her camera out into the too-cold Northeast air.

"What do you see?" May-Bel asks Allison.

"I'm taking pictures," Allison replies. "But you have the camera pointed to the compartment next to us. We need to photograph the compartment after that."

May-Bel tries swinging the camera out a little further. "How is this?" she asks.

"Nope," Allison replies. "All I'm seeing is a reflection off the windows of the compartments."

"Maybe we can see more if we look at the camera screen," I suggest. May-Bel carefully withdraws her selfie stick and camera back into her compartment. We look at the pictures Allison snapped, one by one. No way to see what we want to see. There's too much glare off the windows, and the Shoulders compartment is too far away.

"Look at this!" Allison says. She points to the camera screen, to one of the pictures she's taken. "The windows in the next compartment are all open." I look. They are, from the top, just barely. But I don't get it.

"Are you thinking we can enter the compartment next door and try to take a picture of the Shoulders compartment from there?"

"No," says Allison. "I'm thinking I can use those open windows as tentacle—I mean handholds, and work my way down the outside of the train to see if Gabriel is in the Shoulders compartment."

"What is she saying?" May-Bel asks me.

"She's talking crazy," I sputter. "She thinks she can traverse the outside of the train." Then to Allison. "You've got to be kidding. I'm not going to let you climb out there and get yourself killed."

But Allison is already doing some stretching. Limbering up for this insane maneuver.

"Can you do it?" May-Bel asks. Allison touches her toes and shimmers blue.

"I thththinkkkkk I can," says Allison.

"What? Have you done rock climbing at school?" I sputter some more.

"Some mmmodern dance and tai chi."

"Oh yes!" says May-Bel. "Tai chi is wonderful!"

"If anyone is going to risk their neck here, it's going to be me." I hear my words fall flat as my hand slips off Allison's arm. She slides away from me and just like that she's at the window.

"This window won't open wwwwwwwwwwwide enough for a full-grown man," Allison says, her back turned from me. "It's bbbb-bbbbbbbarely large enough for me."

"She says she can do it," May-Bel says with a certain sense of wonder. "We should be wishing good luck for her. Not arguing."

"I knnnnnnowwww I ccccannnnn ddoooo ittt."

"Do you want to take my camera?" May-Bel asks Allison.

Allison shakes her head no. "I'll need all aaaaaarms free."

"Then take this," May-Bel says, clipping her wireless microphone on Allison's shirt. "Turn it on by pushing the button on the bottom for five seconds. It can record and store eight hours of sound."

Allison extends a long flexible finger and pushes the button as instructed. "I hhhhhope I don't need all eighttttt hours," she says to no one in particular.

"Tell her not to do this," I say to May-Bel. I'm moving towards the window to stop this craziness, but I'm moving too slowly.

It's like walking through water, Inner Mack notices. *Weird.*

"How else can we help?" asks May-Bel. Ignoring me.

"Bbbboth of you, thththink of the sssea."

24

May-Bel videorecords her friend in action

Viewers, you remember the legend of Guanyin helping the Dragon King and becoming a protector of the sea? Well, what if Guanyin's disciples were part sea creatures? Human some of the time and sea creature the other time. Maybe the difference between animal and human is not so big. Perhaps goodness takes on surprising shapes.

This is my friend Allison, opening the window of our train compartment and crawling out and down the side of the train. She moves a little like a giant octopus, does she not? Her motion is smooth, graceful, fluid.

But we know this is an optical illusion because of the camera angle and the filter I am using to shoot this part of the vlog.

I worry that Allison is in danger. But she must find her friend. This is the special meaning of friendship. Friendship is so important. More important than love, even. Friendship makes surprising acts possible.

There she goes! Oh, my heart is pounding so hard. And look at that man looking at her out his window! Oh! Is he surprised! And now

Allison is looking through a different window, trying to see inside. Now she is coming back to us. She looks blue, doesn't she? And her arms look like tentacles! This is a special effect I didn't know the camera had! What beautiful footage of my new special friend.

25

Mack waits and waiting sucks

How long has it been since Allison crawled out the open train window? Well, more like clambered-slid-plopped out, like a gelatinous punk-electric-blue-goth-colored plastic sac squeezing through a space barely large enough to accommodate her tiny body.

Allison asked me to think of the sea. I am trying. The sea I'm thinking of is rough. It is tossing a small lifeboat, and I'm in it, and I'm trying to get Allison in the boat too, but just like what's his name—Leonardo DiCaprio in *Titanic*, she's insisting I stay safe as she remains in the ocean, dealing with the turbulent, freezing waters. But what chance does she have in the storm, a tiny creature at the mercy of wind and water? I close my eyes.

But when I do, the image of raging ocean is replaced by a classic film noir interrogation where I am facing the Representative, and Diamond, and even Shoulders, who press me with accusatory questions. "How could you do that? How could you let that tiny girl climb out a train window to be crushed under the wheels of the train, or sent careening across the gravel mound that supports the train tracks?"

Maybe stop thinking, Inner Mack recommends. I try just watching May-Bel as she leans out her compartment window with her camera, narrating slowly as she records video of Allison doing ... what?

Ludicrously, what leaps to mind is the scene with Bela Lugosi flailing against the non-functional mechanical octopus from *Ed Wood*.

Ok, says Inner Mack. *I guess thinking—in your case—is unavoidable.*

I look back at May-Bel and I feel some comfort—and some jealousy—that she is actually making movies. Movies make sense to me.

Suddenly I picture something I haven't thought about in a long time. I'm sitting on the old sofa in the old house with my dad, watching a movie, and we're both crying. I'm not sure, but the movie might have been *ET*. Now I can see it's a dumb film, but at the time, it really moved me. It really moved US.

I did not cry at my father's funeral. And ever since, I've wondered if there's something fundamentally wrong with me.

Then Allison climbs back through the train window, her hair windblown and spiky, her cheeks flushed and her hands blue from the cold, very much alive.

"You can stop thinking about the sea now," she says.

I cross the compartment ready to kill her.

I hug her instead.

"Allison, for God's sake," I tell her, my head bent so as to speak the words as directly to her as I can ... her pink shell ear being a good foot below my mouth. If I was attracted to her ... this discrepancy in height would be awkward.

Awkward or entrancing? inquires Inner Mack.

Allison breaks free from my hug. "What did you think was going to happen? The train is moving so slowly, I could have practically run alongside it to see into that compartment."

I'm about to argue but May-Bel interjects.

"What did you see?"

"Wwwelll, it looks like there's an extra person in that compartment."

"What do you mean? Who?"

Allison sits down. I could swear that an extra suctioned arm comes out of somewhere and brushes her hair from her face.

"Uh ..." Allison hesitates. She is out of breath. "I guess under those ... conditions ... it's not possible to see through those windows so well. I think they have a tint on them. I can't tell you exactly who I saw. But, six people. Definitely."

"Let me check my video footage," says May-Bel.

We huddle around May-Bel to watch the screen on her little camera. And see ... static. We can barely make out Allison.

"That's strange," mutters May-Bel. "But maybe, if you couldn't see very well, you heard something?"

Allison chuckles. "Not from Shoulders' compartment. But the one before that. A man in there screamed as I passed back and forth across his window."

"Let's listen!" May-Bel says, reaching for the microphone she'd attached to Allison's shirt. Then she frowns, turning the microphone in multiple directions. "It's not switched on," she concludes.

"I could swear I turned it on like you told me to," Allison says.

"Ah yes," says May-Bel dejectedly. "It's this fuzzy wind screen on the microphone. It hides the light that says whether the microphone is on or off."

"So you think I turned it off rather than on?"

"Yes," May-Bel concludes. "It must have been on when I gave it to you. This was my mistake!"

"So if the tech has failed us, we're going to have to use our powers of deduction like Hercule Poirot," I say. But now that Allison is ok, I'm noticing there's not much deduction coming from my brain. I resort to counting people off, one finger at a time. "You said there were six people in the compartment. There's Shoulders. His wife. His kid. The Representative."

Then we hear the Representative in the hallway talking on his cell phone.

"Remember, the Rep wasn't ever sitting with them," Allison says.

"OK, scratch the Representative. Shoulders, his wife and kid, Tiffany, Tirtov and—"

A sixth. Gabriel. Who else could it be?

"We need to get into that compartment," Allison says.

"That's it," I say. "It's time to get the conductor."

But when we exit May-Bel's compartment, the Conductor is already in the hallway. With the Representative.

"While you two were … busy …" begins the Representative, "I took the liberty of reaching out to the conductor, to say that you … that is, we … were suspicious that someone was in Jimmy Shoulders' compartment who didn't belong there."

"Folks, please relax and leave the business of running this train to us." The Conductor looks sternly at me, raises his eyebrows at the kilt, and adjusts his old-timey cap. "But since the Representative is inquiring, I'll let you know that, as it turns out, Mr. Shoulders invited a gentleman to join him in his compartment who only had a second-class ticket. Mr. Shoulders said, this gentleman was ill—"

The Representative interrupts. "I think the exact wording was, 'this lil' feller is feeling right poorly.'"

"In any event ..." The Conductor is growing increasingly annoyed. "We've asked Mr. Shoulders to accompany this gentleman—a Mr. Tirtov—back to second class."

"TIRTOV?" shouts Allison, and we all turn around just in time to see Jimmy Shoulders, or more exactly the back of Jimmy Shoulders, lumbering out of the first-class car for second class. With his arm around a shorter man. Wearing a grey Beatles wig.

"That can't be right!" Allison protests. "Gabriel is the extra person in that compartment." Before the Conductor can stop her, she slides past him and sprints the remaining steps to the compartment of Jimmy Shoulders.

The compartment door is open. Shoulders' wife and son are the only people there. Both asleep.

"Where is everybody?" Allison demands.

The Conductor looks at me like I'm *Ferris Bueller* and he's the Dean of Students. "Sir, you and your party need to calm down. There is an observation car on this train. And a dining car, a number of bathrooms and room in-between cars where people can smoke if they're discrete about it. I'm not here to keep tabs on everyone on a luxury train experience. I *am* here to make certain that this car is reserved for first-class ticket holders. Tickets please." And he extends his hand. Collects a ticket from Allison, then one from May-Bel. He extends his hand to me.

I smile broadly and tilt my teeth to try and catch a brilliant reflection from the available light. And intone with a bit of drawl, "As Jimmy Shoulders might say, I'm just a stranger here myself."

The Conductor is decidedly not amused. "You kids need to understand that this is a vintage train painstakingly restored for the pleasure of passengers who pay for a day of good food and scenery. You are disturbing the operation of this train, the passengers, and me. This ends now." The Conductor points a surprisingly well-manicured finger into my chest. "Please leave first class. You will cease your harassment of everyone here. There are laws governing the operation of trains, and I am an expert in the enforcement of all of them. Please do not test my patience further."

And with that, he gives me a firm shove away from the privileged segment of the train, in the direction of where I belong.

26

May-Bel channels her inner Hercule Poirot

Here are my friends and I walking back to the Observation Car after Mack is told he is not welcome in first class. This has made Allison very angry. She says she does not approve of the class system. No nobles and peasants for Allison! I am happy about this. I like being in the Observation Car with my friends. When I am by myself in my first-class compartment, I think about my husband, and I feel lonely.

It is now time to interview my new close friends, Allison and Mack. Hello friends!

Mack: Hello!

May-Bel: Mack, I see you are drinking a beer.

Mack: Tsingtao. Want one?

May-Bel: Budweiser. Please.

Allison: Hot chocolate. Or Diet Coke. Either one.

Mack: Coming right up!

May-Bel: So Allison ... what is your full name and where do you live?

Allison: May-Bel, would it be ok with you if we just talked?

May-Bel: I think, maybe you want to talk about the mystery of the missing Mr. Gabriel.

Allison: Please.

May-Bel: Sure, but may I record the conversation just for myself? Sometimes I do not understand everything, and it helps me to watch later, and use my voice translation app. Is that ok?

Allison: Yes. I am so worried something bad has happened to my friend Gabriel. I found his ring, found his tin of hot chocolate. And, Gabriel's picture is in the local newspaper. He seems to be everywhere on the train. But wherever I look, he's missing.

May-Bel: I am not a famous detective. But here is what I think. When we first talked, you remembered meeting a man named Mr. Gabriel wearing a ring. So we thought, maybe you imagined him. But now there are many clues you really saw him.

Allison: Also ... people seem so certain that Gabriel doesn't exist. Why wouldn't they say, we don't know? Why not say, we're not sure?

May-Bel: In a detective story, when everyone says that one person is wrong, that is a clue. That the one person is right.

Allison: Didn't you say earlier that sometimes everyone is right and the one person is wrong?

May-Bel: But this is a mystery. The rules are different.

Allison: Hey, where is Mack with our drinks? Do you see him?

May-Bel: No.

Allison: Uh ... why are you smiling like that?

May-Bel: You like him, I think.

Allison: Who? Mack? I do not!

May-Bel: We are friends, right? Friends should be honest. It is obvious. The way you look at him. The way you argue with him.

Allison: He is such a jerk.

May-Bel: I am a married lady, so I have learned many things. Soon, the train ride will be over. Mack will go someplace else, play the pipes. Will you tell Mack the jerk you like him before he goes?

Mack: Who's a jerk?

May-Bel: Oh!

Mack: Here's your beer, May-Bel. They didn't have Budweiser, so I got you Guinness. And a Diet Pepsi for you, Allison.

Allison: I ordered Diet Coke.

Mack: Same thing.

Allison: They're not the … oh … I am not going to argue with you.

Mack: What's May-Bel smiling at?

Allison: I don't know. She's been doing that a lot lately.

May-Bel: Allison was asking why it took so long to get the drinks?

Mack: Sorry about that. I took a little detour. I went to second class to make sure my bagpipes are still there. And while I was there, I had a talk with Jimmy Shoulders.

May-Bel: Is he going to perform later?

Mack: He promised he would, but you never know with celebrities. You know, that Tirtov guy with him didn't look so good. He was slumped in his seat next to Shoulders, and he seemed kind of out of it. He kept muttering the same two words over and over in Russian.

May-Bel: Will Mr. Shoulders get Mr. Tirtov to a doctor?

Mack: That's not exactly what Shoulders said.

Allison: What exactly *did* he say?

Mack: Shoulders said the ol' feller would feel right as rain once he had a sip of the Texas medicine brewed up by his Missus. And then Shoulders poured what looked like a quart of homebrew out of a canteen directly into Tirtov's mouth.

Allison: Fascinating, but while you were away May-Bel said she agrees with me that Gabriel is real and still on this train.

May-Bel: No ... I said, I think you did not imagine Gabriel on this train. But I do not know if he is still here.

Allison: Not here? Then where would he be?

May-Bel: I think we have to be logical detectives. Let's guess Gabriel came on the train with Allison, then he was captured by bad people and taken to the baggage car. Let's guess he escaped, accidentally leaving his ring behind in a hurry.

Mack: But if Gabriel escaped, why would he stay on the train? Why not leave to go someplace safe?

Allison: If he'd escaped, I think we would have seen him. We've been watching every time the train stopped. No, I think he's still on the train, and the bad guys moved him out of the baggage car when they realized we were looking for him.

Mack: That still leaves us where we started, wondering where the hell he is.

May-Bel: And wondering, who are the bad guys?

Mack: I don't like Shoulders.

Allison: Or that Tiffany woman, whoever she is.

Mack: I think maybe Congressman Joe did it all by himself.

Allison: For fuck's sake, the Congressman is the only person on this train trying to help us!

May-Bel: Oh, the train is stopping. We are pulling into a station. Please wait, Allison and Mack. I need to create some content for my vlog.

Mack: Weren't you recording just now?

May-Bel: Yes, but just for myself. This will be for my audience.

Allison: That's ok. Mack and I want to keep a close eye on what goes on at this station, who gets on and off the train.

Hello dear viewers! This is May-Bel again, your Happy Train Vlogger. We are now coming to our second stop on this special train, in the town of Hoosick Falls. This is a funny name for a town. Who is sick? I don't know!

The depot building looks very old, with grey brickwork and a steep grey slate roof. There are also many windows, but there are drapes drawn in each window, and there seems to be a wire fence around the building. I think the building is closed. I do not see anyone inside. But you can see many people on the platform, waiting to get on our train. I wish I had time to exit the train at all these pretty little towns and learn more about what the United States is like.

Let's go over to the window so we can see the town more clearly.

27

Mack loses the girl, again

As we pull into Hoosick Falls, Allison and I take our usual positions to see who gets on and off the train. This time Allison takes the side facing the depot and I take the other side, overlooking a small parking lot and the town beyond it. Hoosick Falls looks like every other burg on this voyage: picturesque, if by picturesque you mean old, neglected and depressing.

Allison yells, "Hey Mack, come check this out." I cross the observation car to see ... Shoulders get off the train with Tirtov. Tirtov is needing a lot of assistance—he isn't walking so well. They blend into the usual assortment of day-tourists on the platform ready to board.

May-Bel joins us at the window. "Is that Mr. Shoulders out there?" she asks us. "Why is he leaving the train?"

"Maybe to get Tirtov to a doctor," I suggest.

"I am having trouble seeing them," May-Bel says, on tip-toes. "Here, stick my camera high on the window, use the suction cup. I can get better video with the camera up high. Do you have it pointed at Mr. Tirtov?"

"Yes," I assure her.

May-Bel sighs. "I am disappointed. I guess Mr. Shoulders will not perform a song for us."

"No, look again," says Allison. "Shoulders is getting back on the train."

He is. He's left Tirtov sitting by himself, on a bench on one edge of the depot. "Shoulders shouldn't have dumped him there," I think aloud.

"Why not?" May-Bel asks.

"Tirtov's completely out of it. He kept saying the same two words in Russian, over and over. And I don't think that's enough to get him an Uber to the nearest medical center."

"How do you know he was speaking Russian?" Allison asks suddenly.

I sigh. Is this going to be another ridiculous argument?

"What else would he be speaking but Russian? He kept on saying something weird like 'tut vey tut vey.'"

"Say that again slowly."

"Toot vay toot vay."

Allison jumps and punches my arm.

"Ouch!" I say.

"You overeducated dope," she yells. "That's not Russian, that's Yiddish—it means THAT HURTS."

"It sure does," I say back, rubbing my arm. For a petite person she certainly packs a wallop. "What's your point? Why would Tirtov speak Yiddish?"

But she is already heading to the other end of the train. AKA the exit.

There she goes, says Inner Mack. *Again.*

"Why would Tirtov speak Yiddish?" I ask her as I walk after her.

"Because—look—he's even wearing teal socks."

"Who is?"

"I've got to get off this train!" is her answer.

This time I'm fast enough to grab her shoulder.

"Wait a minute!" I tell her. I can hear May-Bel behind me, speaking rapidly in Chinese.

Allison struggles to get free of my grip. "Gabriel wore teal socks."

I still don't get it. "Anyone can wear teal socks."

"And anyone can wear a grey Beatles wig," she says, finally breaking free of my grip. She races to the door of the observation car, me following but not quickly enough. She jumps off the train just after it starts moving.

The train turns a corner, and the station is out of view. I turn back to the observation car, and May-Bel is there.

"I think Allison has found her Gabriel," she tells me.

28

Tirtov plots his next move

"Idiot!" I tell Shoulders. "You had one job. Hold onto Gabriel Solomon. Keep him safe and secure on this train."

This wild west man Shoulders slumps sloppily in his seat. "Tirtov, I thought he was gonna die. I didn't want him croakin' on us. I thought, get the lil' dude some air. Maybe he needed a smoke."

I cannot believe I'm here wasting my time with this moron. I cannot wait to return to my dacha in Connecticut. Still, the westerner deserves a good tongue-lashing. Which I give him right here in our compartment. In front of his wife and child, who remain silent and motionless. In front of this blonde cut to look like the former President's daughter—who continues to type away on her tablet as if nothing is happening.

"You say you intended to bring Solomon back onto the train?" I ask him.

"That's what I *was* doing," he replies, wide-eyed. He is truly a stupid and uninteresting example of the type of people one must work with these days. Give me an old-fashioned oligarch's henchman any day.

"I was half-way back to the train and I took my eyes off him for just a moment. How was I supposed to figger that little gal was gonna snatch him?"

I laugh scornfully. "You expect me to believe that? You, a grown man? Outsmarted by a tiny girl?"

Shoulders sits up like straight like a little boy attempting to defend his cheating on a test at school. "Hey that ain't fair!" he squawks. "She's quick as a sidewinder and twice as hard to see comin'."

Without my wig I look like the actor Yul Brynner. I put my hand on my hips the way he did in *The King and I*, and attempt to look at once disgusted and imposing—easy. I stand up in our compartment, because that is even more magisterial. I lurch periodically with the train in what I hope is a threatening manner.

"So you—the famed gunslinger and rodeo champion—were defeated by her and ran?" I ask rhetorically.

Shoulders bows his head. He goes from pompous to abject with incredible speed, I must say.

"I didn't have time to do nothin' else."

Something seems to occur to Shoulders. It's comical to see an idea take shape in that thick skull and gradually make it through his speech center to form actual words. "Damn it all, Tirtov," he says. "You got people on the outside who can handle a drugged ol' communist and a teeny-bopper goth, can't they?"

I smile, showing my quite expensive dentures. "Shoulders, they can handle an ersatz fifth columnist country singer, too."

Shoulders returns to his abject schoolboy position in his seat. "Now, let's not say nothin' we don't mean. We're sitting fine. Gabriel's time is up, sure as shootin'. Your people will git him, or someone else's will, or the feds will grab him. And whatever comes ... kudos, reward money, just like we planned, we split it even."

Finally, the cowboy utters a sensible observation.

"Indeed, ahem partner. We split evenly. With those who remain."

29

Diamond reconsiders her options

I've had it out with Russell, or as out as I'm going to have it. I sit in the observation car, I stop drinking and I just write.

I write about me and Russell, about what's been happening on the train, and about the wrestlers—those funny guys dressed in cheap suits. I write about DanieLa, about myself and how weird the MFA experience has been, about the skinny little white Goth girl and the boy in the kilt, and how in America we're continually trying to self-reinvent, or re-self-invent, or however you want to put those three things together. I write about how I would like to be loved or even liked as a person, and how being a Black woman is a lot of work.

Is being a Chinese woman a lot of work? It probably is. A different sort of work, but probably a lot of work all the same. I wonder if I went to China, how I would be treated. As someone special or something strange? A part of me would like to go and find out. At least I won't get shot in China. The convo with the Chinese woman about guns was crazy. But interesting. China and its enormous history of poetry. The Book of Songs and the Tang Poets and the contemporary poets.

A lot of them women. A lot of them women poets from the get-go. Who told me all that? Russell.

Why do smart people, with so much knowledge, have to be such bastards? Why is gathering the learning nuggets such a trial? Why is there so much potential poison in learning? I don't know. I just keep writing.

And as I write it all hits me—the Doubt. Do I really want to jettison someone who has helped me and who *will* help me, probably? Is this really smart?

I like Russell, I like the sex, I like the way he makes me feel. Until I don't. He will introduce me to a publisher. He is as good as his word—at least as far as the writing goes. Then Doubt takes on all the voices of my older female relatives, drowning me out. Be careful, take care of yourself, don't upset anybody who might be able to help you. Do what you have to do to survive. And then, in the background is DanieLa, saying quietly, Sis, is this really what you want? Is this what's going to nourish you? Don't you deserve someone who loves you and commits to you and who doesn't have a wife and family? Isn't this a compromise that kills?

I keep on writing. I talk to Doubt and all of Doubt's mothers and aunts. But DanieLa stays with me through the whole multivocal conversation. Diminished sometimes, sometimes imperfectly heard, but still there: a low persistent tone under all the noise. A voice that won't be drowned out completely. Like Tina, like Beyoncé, like Maya, like all of our singers—like Sudan Archives singing in a studio she built in her basement with her boyfriend, to make and produce those tunes on her own. Doing it all on a shoestring. Playing that African violin. Unintimidated by the world.

30

An Uber driver gets a surprising passenger

So this really old guy with a grey wig gets into my car, and first I think he's sitting with a girl, but then I notice he's actually sitting with this giant blue octopus.

Now it's true—you see all kinds of things driving an Uber, but this was really something well, out of the ordinary. I mean you don't often see a guy that old wearing a Beatles wig that big just doing Uber and acting all chill about it ... I mean, a lot of old people don't know how to use the app, so it was crazy that he understood the tech. The octopus seemed very at home in the taxi, which isn't surprising because they can really get used to anything. If you've seen *My Octopus Teacher* you know that, right?

Anyway, but the man! That was crazy!!! The old people really can surprise you, you know. I think old people are really boring usually, but this guy wanted to know all about what I was studying and reading—not that I read much—and he wanted to know what I was up to, and when he found out I was originally from Korea, he wanted to know all about my family and what kind of food we liked to make for dinner, and how we liked living in America and were we satisfied with how the government was treating us—which I thought was a very considerate question, although it made me a little uncomfortable, because you never know.

All this time the octopus was nodding and I guess had been trained to speak. Again, not surprising—they're really smart. It was saying things like please gggggo faster ... which I appreciated because I for one love shredding in my Tesla even though as the octopus reminded me, Elon MMMMMMMusk is a mmmmmadman. Point taken, but the price of the car just went down so what's a person to do? I mean, you know?

But it was a bit funny that I picked them up at the train station, and then they wanted to be dropped off at another train station.

"Not to worry, young lady," the old guy said to his octopus. "We'll catch up with the train at Moretz."

"Had to make an unscheduled stop?" I asked.

"Yesssssss," said the octopus. "I haddddd to say hellooooooo ttttto an oldddd ffriend."

31

Mack says goodbye and hello

I stare out the window of the observation car, now that Allison is gone, and wonder how anyone endures a winter in the American Northeast. We are travelling through countryside that must be lush and green for much of the year, but in winter's dreary light it's hard to fathom how nature could be so devoid of color. How living things can exist solely in shades of grey and still be … living things.

In one corner of the observation car, May-Bel sits and fiddles with her camera equipment. Perhaps she's editing footage for her vlog. Across from her, Diamond sits typing on her MacBook. A poet, she says she was. Or is. I think just about every girl I dated wrote poetry. I don't think any of them were poets.

I somehow doubt Allison writes poetry. Which is refreshing. Or would be if she hadn't gotten off the train without saying goodbye.

I never liked goodbyes anyway, because the ones in real life never measure up to the movies. I mean, how about a goodbye like the one Rick (Humphrey Bogart) and Ilsa (Ingrid Bergman) share in *Casablanca*? They're at the exotic airport, the plane she's about to board with her husband has its propellers turning, she desperately wants to abandon her husband and have crazy sex in Casablanca with Rick (not in the script, but it's implicit, right?), then Bogy says she must get on the plane. Ingrid is more beautiful than anyone has a right to be on a tarmac, and she weeps lustrously as she tells him, "God bless you," turns to board the plane as it pulls away, and then he's off to save the world from Hitler along with Claude Rains. *That's* a goodbye.

Unlike the one I had with Elizabeth, where I had the feeling she knew things were over between us well before she ran the final credits. The goodbye she said to me out loud was a ritual she performed long after some farewell she'd rehearsed silently, to herself. And she sure didn't say "God bless you" when she walked out.

Why are you obsessing over this goodbye detail when you insist repeatedly that you don't even like Allison, asks Inner Mack, with that "see I told you so" intonation that is particularly infuriating in an inner voice.

May-Bel is waving in my direction. I must be throwing off some kind of sadness musk. I go over to see what she wants.

"I guess the mystery is over, huh?" I tell her, trying to sound like I'm ok with that.

But she continues to wave me closer. She's looking at the video screen on the back of her camera. I peer at it too. The screen is maybe four inches in diagonal, and I can't see much detail, because May-Bel seems to be using a wide frame of view and the screen shows just about the entire platform of the station we just left. May-Bel advances quickly through the footage, to the point where the platform clears and there are just two remaining figures moving slowly away from the train.

"Allison and Gabriel?" I ask her. She nods.

"I can zoom in," she says, and she spreads two fingers apart on the video screen to narrow the view. The figures on screen are Allison and Gabriel all right. I can tell from Allison's messenger bag and Gabriel's teal socks. He has a lot of sock showing. Old men and their high-water pants.

"Now watch this," May-Bel instructs me. I see the two figures exit the platform and cross to one side of the depot. The camera's point of view moves from right to left, following what the camera saw as our train pulled out of the station—but the camera's wide field of view keeps Allison and Gabriel on screen as they enter a car. The car does not appear to be a taxi. Probably a Lyft or Uber.

And following right behind them are two broad-shouldered men in dark suits. They appear to be entering a second car as the camera loses sight of the station.

"Who the hell are they?" I ask loudly. May-Bel reverses the direction of the footage and replays it. Even with May-Bel's fancy equipment, it's hard to see the men in any detail.

"Secret Police," May-Bel whispers. And I'm about to explain that this isn't China and we don't have secret police, when I think about plain-clothed police, undercover narcotics agents, FBI sting operations and whatever the CIA might be doing that it's not supposed to do. Not to mention, the folks Representative Joe had in mind when he said that Gabriel might not be safe on this train. So I just nod at May-Bel. Secret Police is as good a shorthand as any.

"Our friend Allison is in trouble," May-Bel says, in the same whisper.

32

Tiffany Tolliver grabs some Presidential face-time

I'm calling to report on the operation but first.

Look at me, Daddy, I mean Mr. President.

No, I mean it. Look at me. See how blonde I am now? See how small my nose is? See how good my body is?

Yes, now listen, sir, we—

Have a situation here but I'm fixing it.

Don't worry—I can handle the problem! I'm a lawyer now!

I have a head for business!

I can learn this other part too.

No, I'm not saying I'm smarter than you.

I never said that, I would NEVER even THINK that.

Just remember, among your kids and their doubles, I'm the smart one.

And now I'm a pretty one too.

I look just like your real daughters!

After the improvements.

Thank you.

Yes, all the action is being recorded.

Yes, we KNOW you like to watch, not read.

Yes, it IS a familiar story!

You're so brilliant!

This is just the raw footage. Of course, sir.

Whatever you say.

Could you look at me just one more time?

Look hard.

33

Mack is back on the case

I've placed my phone on the table between me and May-Bel, and I'm thinking about what to do to protect Allison—and Gabriel—from the "secret police" that are probably following them right now to ... wherever Allison is taking Gabriel. A hospital, probably. I'm so deep in thought, I don't notice my phone is buzzing. Or that May-Bel has picked it up. Or that she's reading my messages. Not until she interrupts me with:

"This message is for you."

She smiles and hands me my phone. It's a new message thread from a 413 area code. It begins:

> Hey Kilt Boy, I'm not done with you yet.

Allison.

> Answer me, motherfucker

There's more:

> I AM SO GOING TO KILL
> YOU THE NEXT TIME I
> SEE YOU

I type quickly.

> I'm here

The reply is almost instant.

> About fucking time. I need
> your help

Huh?

> How? Are you and Gabriel
> at the hospital?

> He won't go to the hospital.
> He wants back on the train

> What? Why?

> Don't ask questions. He says he promised someone he'd stay on the train.

I'm trying to figure out, how does Allison even have my cell phone number?

> How do you even have my cell phone number?

> You asked me to text you my lunch selfie. Did you think I wasn't on to that?

Damn.

I think I better mention the secret police.

> You know, you're being followed.

> ? I don't see anyone

I start to type an explanation, but Allison's next message arrives first.

> Focus, pipe brain. The next train stop is Moretz

I think a second. Then type:

> You can't just get back on the train in Moretz. Everyone will see you. Gabriel's cover will be blown

> I know that. That's where you come in

Me?

> How?

> Figure something out so we can sneak on unobserved

May-Bel asks if she can text something to Allison. I need a moment to think anyway, so I hand May-Bel my phone. In a moment she hands it back to me. With the following exchange added:

> Hi, this is your friend May-Bel. Can I call him Kilt-Boy too or is that a love name? ;*)

> FFS

I don't know why *I'm* kilt-boy. There must be thirty guys on this train wearing kilts.

Which gives me an idea.

> I got an idea.

> I'll alert CNN

> When does the train arrive in Moretz?

> 10 minutes. What's the idea?

> Shit. 10 mins not much. No time to explain. Just don't show up early in Moretz. 1 minute late is good

> What's the plan?

> Just get there when I said

34

Mack—wait for it—asks for help

To make my plan work, I need help. I excuse myself to May-Bel and go find the Representative, who is moving swiftly from the other direction. We practically collide in the hallway in second class.

"I need to talk to you," I say to Joe.

"But I need to speak with you first," he insists. "To you and Allison, actually."

I'm taken aback by that one. "Um, she's not available right now."

"I'm aware," says Joe in his best soap opera voice. "She's with Gabriel."

He's worrisomely smart sometimes, isn't he? observes Inner Mack.

"So you finally believe us about Gabriel."

"Stop wasting time," he says. "The two of them are not on this train. Where are they?"

I tell him something close to the truth. "I don't know where they are."

Then Joe says something surprising. "You need to get them back on."

I shake my head at this. "You said Gabriel being on this train could put him in danger."

Joe nods. "He's in danger wherever he is." He leans towards me, after looking up and down the hallway. "Look, I don't have time to explain, so just trust me. Gabriel has a lot of enemies. More than I expected. If you get him back on this train, I can be responsible for him. Out there," Joe waves his hand at the window, "I can't vouch for what happens to him, or to our friend Allison."

I look out the window, at the everlasting winter. It's starting to look better to me. You can capture a lot just in shades of black and white.

"Ok, Joe, I'll do what you ask, but I need five minutes at our next stop."

Joe seems insulted to be asked to do something in some small way useful. "You want me to hold up the train?" he asks.

I put my hand on Joe's shoulder. "Get me five minutes after we arrive in Moretz, and before the train pulls out of the station. I'd ask the conductor myself, but for some reason he doesn't seem fond of me."

Now it's Joe who seems uncertain. "Even if I can manage to get the delay ... how is five minutes going to help you?"

"I don't have time to explain. Just trust me."

35

May-Bel records an impromptu concert

Hello dear viewers, May-Bel here as our special train pulls into the tiny town of Moretz. Our friend Mack the kilt-boy has promised us something special at this stop, and look! Even before the train comes to a halt, all the men in kilts are jumping off the train, and Mack is leading them. They all have their bagpipes with them ... and now Mack is shouting to us, we're going to hear a rare pipe orchestra performance of "My Way" by Frank Sinatra.

And ... wow.

This is loud.

I don't know how this music will sound on the vlog, so let me describe it, if you can hear me. The music has this loud continuous humming sound, so loud that the windows of the train are vibrating. My back teeth are vibrating! Above the humming is a melody, with very few notes, and the melody is so high-pitched and piercing, it blends with the humming.

It is ... strikingly beautiful.

But also, crazy! Look at all the bagpipe players marching around the train platform. Some are marching in and out of the train depot! Even the ones who aren't moving back and forth are marching in place. Some even crash into each other, laugh, and go on marching. I don't think they practiced this!

Mack explained this to me a moment ago. The bagpipe has three big pipes called drones that play one sound each, and a fourth pipe called a chanter that can play nine notes. All the pipes are attached to a bag of air, and the player squeezes the bag to blow air through the pipes and make the music. There is a fifth pipe the player uses to blow air into the bag to keep it inflated.

It is interesting, the bagpipe always plays at the same volume and the music is continuous. It does not start or stop. It just ... goes until it is finished.

Did I say, this is loud? Some people crowd near me by the train window here in the observation car. They are smiling, trying to get as close as they can to the music. Other people in the car have backed against the other wall and have their hands covering their ears. Not everyone likes the bagpipes! Representative Joe, the former member of the U.S. government, is crouched below a table with his head between his knees. He is not a fan of Mack's music!

But I am enjoying the music very much. It is loud like a rock band with the volume turned up. You cannot get away from the music! It takes over your senses and your whole body.

And look who is back on the train! It is my friend Allison.

Allison: Hey, sister!

May-Bel: I am so glad to see you safe.

Allison: What?

May-Bel: I am glad you are safe!

Allison: Yes, this is great! So loud! Who knew Mack could do anything this cool?

May-Bel: Where is Gabriel?

Allison: What?

May-Bel: YOUR FRIEND GABRIEL!

Allison: Shh! Not so loud! Someone will hear you ... he's out there somewhere. With the bagpipers.

Then suddenly the music stops. Only not really. It's still there, in the ringing in my ears. Everyone is cheering and jumping up and down. Except of course the people who didn't like the music. They are shaking their heads and talking to each other, frowning.

The conductor calls "ALL ABOARD." It is time for the train to leave. The music lovers on the train are still applauding loudly. The bagpipers are coming back on the train, laughing and hugging.

And with the applause at its loudest, Mr. Shoulders comes over to me. He wants to do his concert right away!

Shoulders: I think I'll play that song for you now, while everybody's hankerin' for some real music. Before the train leaves, so the people on the platform can hear, too.

May-Bel: Oh! This is so exciting. Where should I set up my camera?

Shoulders: Over here. On a tripod on this table. I'll be standing out here, on the balcony at the back of the observation car. What are you using for a microphone?

May-Bel: I have two microphones. They are wireless.

Shoulders: Thare's perfect. I'll just clip one to my guitar, like this. And the other on my lapel. You can mix the music and voice later. Now ... what am I gonna do with this baby while I play?

Mr. Shoulders is spinning his six-shooter gun on one finger, like a real movie cowboy. And now ... oh dear, he is handing me the gun.

Shoulders: Why don't you take care of this for me, while I sing a song for all the folks back in Communist China.

The gun is polished to a mirror-like shine, and it is surprisingly heavy, at least a kilogram I guess. I don't know how anyone holds this gun steady to hit the target.

Shoulders: You shouldn't be af'erd of guns, little lady. They keep us free. You make sure you tell that to your kinfolk back home.

36

Jimmy sings and takes a dirt nap

Here is the final performance in the career of Jimmy Shoulders, as recorded by May-Bel and performed for the passengers in the observation car and local townspeople gathered on the Moretz train platform.

"Thank you, thank you kindly, ladies and gents. That's right nice of you. I've got one more number I'd like to sing for you all, and this song has treated me kindly, you might say. Just as Jesus Christ has treated me kindly, given this ol' sinner eternal life. I'd like to sing a song about Jesus, who is not just my Lord and Savior but my friend and constant companion. If you know the words, you can just sing along, or clap your hands or stomp your feet, or if you're drinking anything stronger than root beer, you can try rattlin' your ice cubes."

He strums his guitar to make sure it's in tune.

A rodeo star's life is thrillin'
Filled with purty gals with no remorse
But when the sun goes down
The show ends, the crowd's gone
In the dark there's just me and my horse

On the range I get mighty lonely
The cold moon shining blue all night long
'Neath the dark prairie skies
And the night's thousand eyes
I think 'bout all my lapses and wrongs

Cowboy's lives ain't so fascinatin'
The wages of sin keep us sleepless
When the coyotes yowl
Then it's me that'll howl
Calling for my bronc buster Jesus

Now, Jesus is my kind of cowboy
His word is where you've gotta start
I'm telling you, par'd
Put your faith in the Lord
And he'll shoot his truth straight through your heart

A SHOT RINGS OUT.

MAY-BEL'S AUDIO FEED ENDS HERE.

37

Mack confronts death (someone else's)

We crowd against the large window at the end of the observation car—those of us who could get there first—as this pretend-antique, old-timey train grinds to a start and then screeches to a halt in a field north of the Moretz station. Jimmy Shoulders lies on the floor of the little balcony on the outside end of the car, where he was performing for May-Bel and the rest of us. Half his body seems to be hanging off the train, even though the little balcony is fully enclosed in a low black ironwork fence designed to keep bodies—that is, live bodies—from falling out.

When someone lies motionless in the movies pretending to be dead, the pretense works, like it's impossible to tell if someone has been killed or is just sleeping soundly unless you do something like poke them with a bayonet. But I don't need a bayonet with Jimmy; no one would.

May-Bel holds Jimmy's six-shooter loosely against her hip. The gun looks as much like a prop as when Jimmy handed it to May-Bel. It seems impossible to me that she could have pulled its trigger, and just as impossible that the gun would have fired if she had. Yet there she is. And there he is.

Where is Allison?

Possibly she is easing her way back through the crowd, in that liquid way of hers, towards the bagpipers, who characteristically are congregated around the bar, where they were when the shot was fired. Somewhere in that mess of plaid is Gabriel, wearing my spare kilt and going along with my cockamamie plan.

Yes ... concealing Gabriel among the bagpipers seemed like a great idea at the time, but like most of my great ideas, it came to me without much in the way of accompanying detail. Like, how to get him into a kilt ... I had to improvise that one. And, what to do with his pants once he changed into my kilt? Well ... those pants are sitting on the floor of the men's room in the Moretz station depot, if he ever wants to go back there to try and retrieve them. I probably should have considered, this poor guy can't be expected to run around Canada in my spare kilt. At some point, he's going to have to beg or borrow a new pair of old man's pants. But, hey. At least I had the presence of mind to grab his wallet and keys from his old pants and stuff them in my sporran, before we returned to the train platform to blend in with the other bagpipers.

No one moves towards May-Bel, and no one flees in the opposite direction. It feels like an awful amount of time passing just like that, all of us figures in a kind of frozen snow globe, waiting for someone to pick us up and shake.

I look around for Jimmy's wife and kid. They have had oodles of time to run forward, screaming. I don't see or hear them.

38

Diamond admires May-Bel's presence of mind

May-Bel has barely moved since the shot was fired. Her face is obscured by the reflection off the glass back of the observation car. The light gleams off the pistol she's carrying.

The two wrestlers stand crowded next to me, on my right side. I can eavesdrop on part of their conversation. "We can't afford to be late into Canada," one of them says. "We can't just let her hang," says the other. Meaning May-Bel, I suppose. "But she's certainly keeping her cool."

I wonder, what do mothers in China teach their children? About the law, and when you're caught on the other side? Would I be as silent and still as this girl, if (say) I were pulled over by police in a small town in Alabama, or Oklahoma, or hell, in Vermont? I've got a broken headlight and a blunt I've just put out on the floor mat, and here comes the state trooper, face obscured by the dark, the brim of his hat and the bright of a flashlight about two feet long.

No, I wouldn't be this self-possessed.

"I called the police," says the Representative from somewhere behind me. "Everyone stay right where they are. Don't touch anything." I almost laugh. This dude is taking charge? There are—how many of us?—crowded into this observation car? All to hear Jimmy Shoulders sing.

The Representative moves smoothly through the crush of people in the car until he reaches the back where May-Bel is standing.

"Please hand me that gun," he tells her. He holds a pencil towards her. And, bless May-Bel, she hands the pistol to the Representative upside-down, so that the pistol hangs from the pencil by its trigger guard. She must have watched American police procedurals, to know that trick. He slips the gun into a side pocket of his suit jacket. He kneels for a moment, to get a better look at the body of Jimmy Shoulders, then pivots to face the rest of us.

"My name is Joe Salvatorre, the former Congressman from the district where we're stopped for the moment," he announces in a firm and confident voice. "I will have to ask you to obey my instructions until law enforcement arrives. Please, clear the aisle so that first responders can move as needed through this car."

No one cries bullshit. This Representative, recently rejected by the voters, is now our supreme leader. And the other white men in the room have sniffed the air and decided for the rest of us, yes. He rules.

"We have to get out of here, find another way to Canada," says Russell to me quietly. Without my noticing, he has parked himself against my left elbow. "There's a guy with a pistol guarding the other end of the train. Bald as a melon, wearing—get this—an ascot with a pearl pin."

Before I can respond he is pushing forward to say something to the Representative, who first shakes his head, then nods.

With me, Russell is Armenian-American. Or claims to be. Standing with the Representative ... he's just one white man talking to another.

May-Bel stands off to one side. Disarmed, she is forgotten. For the moment, at least.

39

May-Bel can't vlog the scene before her

This is terrible. There is a dead cowboy just a meter from my feet. I know from watching Western movies, I should not make any "sudden moves." I would like to bend over Mr. Shoulders, so he has someone with him. But I cannot do that safely. I cannot reach my video camera, which is pointed towards where Mr. Shoulders was standing. Not where he is lying now.

Mr. Shoulders has my wireless microphones. I cannot even record my own voice right now. The police will take Mr. Shoulders away. I will never get those microphones back.

I wanted to meet a cowboy. I think long ago there was a real cowboy who was handsome and brave. He was a model for other cowboys, who pretended to be like the real cowboy. Now no one can remember the real cowboy, only the pretend ones that came after. Cowboys like Mr. Shoulders just pretend to be pretend.

The biggest moment in my vlogging career, and I am missing the whole thing. My viewers will be so disappointed.

40

The Kid stays one step ahead of Death (again)

The nice woman pretending to be my mother wears a long coat that reaches nearly to the floor. She has buttoned me inside, facing her.

She tells me, the man pretending to be my father is dead. I am not surprised. Death follows me. It will catch up to me, too. But not today, I tell myself.

The nice woman tells me, we must move to a new location on the train, where I can hide until it is safe. I nod. Maybe she can feel me nod when my forehead bumps against her rib cage. I do not take up much room inside her coat.

We are in motion. I have my arms around her waist, my legs around hers. I am strong. I can stay motionless as she carries me forward. Motion feels good; I have been in motion ever since I left my real mother and father in Nicaragua. "Stay safe," they told me. "We are counting on you. We will all be together soon. In the United States. Or Canada." They were crying. I did not cry. I tried to be brave. For them.

The nice woman stops moving. She is speaking to some men, in a language I don't understand. The language is not English. I am frightened. I cannot let anyone see how frightened I am. I remember the words of an old woman who rode with me and many others in the back of a truck as we crossed the border into Mexico. "Sometimes you must stand strong, little one," she told me in a firm quiet voice that reminded me of my grandmother. "And sometimes you must let the wind take hold of you like a fallen leaf. Like a hawk carried ever higher by an updraft."

Hands—men's hands—take hold of me. The nice woman tells me not to be afraid. She will come for me soon. Or if not her, then the man. The kind man in the photograph she gave me. I nod again.

The men's hands place me on the floor facing a large refrigerator. The refrigerator door is open. The hands slide open a door in the bottom of the refrigerator, and explain in English that there is space underneath the refrigerator for me to hide. Other boys my age have hidden there before, they say. There is a vent with air for me to breathe. I will be safe there.

I crawl into the space. It is smaller than they say. The hands close the door above my head. I make myself as small as I can. I have been shut in before. I have been this cold before.

I think of the face of the woman who pretended to be my mother on the train. It is a nice face. I think of the face of the man in the photograph she gave me, the man she says will take care of me if she cannot. His is a nice face too, with glasses and a plaid scarf wrapped around his neck. I have never seen this man except in the photograph. But I think if this man comes, I will recognize him by his scarf.

I close my eyes tight for a moment, and think of a hawk in the wind. I think of my real mother and father. They are counting on me.

I breathe.

41

The Representative's secret plan

So Much Winning

The Innermost Thoughts of Joe Salvatorre,
(Former[future]) Representative

U.S. House of Representatives (NY CD-21)

Presented as Powerpoint

Plan prepared on the Voyages Retro Train to Merveilleux City, Canada

Checklist for Success on the Train

- Tirtov (check!). So Much Hate
  - Old Russian hate for Jews and Muslims
  - New American-acquired hate for people of color and anyone remotely gay
  - Special hate for immigrants
  - Runs posse like the one run by Shoulders—see next card
  - Believes in the Three Rs: retribution, retaliation and revenge
  - WARNING: caution advised! He's reputed to have connections to the Russian Mafia (murder ... and worse)

Checklist for Success on Train (Cont'd)

- Shoulders (check!)
  - Con man and B-list Christian cowboy "entertainer"
  - Long on muscle; short on brains
  - Works with armed vigilantes patrolling the Texas-Mexico border looking to rough up immigrants crossing illegally
  - **Shoulders and Tirtov forming an alliance of posse leaders**

- Two wrestlers (check!)
  - Both with immigration issues
  - Independent, unionizing, *not* liked by corporate management
  - ~~Tirtov's target (murder? arrest? abduction?)~~

Checklist for Success on Train (Cont'd)

- ** Gabriel Solomon - **Our New Target**
  - Surprise! His presence on train was unexpected!
  - I am extraordinarily nimble. I can change plans
  - The New Plan: Hold Solomon on train until Homeland Security can arrest him
    - Take credit for his arrest (press coverage will help my campaign)
    - Claim the reward for his arrest—split it with Tirtov ~~and Shoulders~~ (Tiffany also?)

Checklist for Success on Train (Cont'd)

- Tiffany Tolliver (another unplanned presence—Lucky?)
  - There must be a way for me to take advantage of her connection with the former President
  - *(what is that connection?) (who the hell is she?)*
- May-Bel (lucky again!) This is great because:
  - She hosts an online travel vlog with half a million followers in China
  - Her father is an oligarch who's made millions selling flooring supplies to Home Depot
  - $$$$$$ = 👊👊👊👊👊

A Brief Aside: Who Shot Shoulders?

- Could have been anyone
  - Tirtov's people
  - Tiffany's people
  - His own people

- Why was Shoulders shot?
  - They asked him to kill Gabriel Solomon and he didn't
  - They asked him not to kill Gabriel, were afraid he would anyway
  - To get his share of the reward for the arrest of Gabriel
  - He intentionally removed Gabriel from the train? (Going rogue?)
  - I don't know!

What's In It For Me

- Publicity
- Money
  - From Tirtov -> Russian Mafia
  - ~~From Shoulders~~
  - From May-Bel and her father
  - **There's never enough money, especially for the elections I want to win. The BIG ones**

It's Better to be Lucky than Good

- **Shoulders dead and Solomon alive? Crazy!!**
  - Tirtov meant to kill Solomon after having him abducted under goth girl's nose (the incident over the cocoa)
  - But Solomon was saved when Tiffany and I saw the local news article offering a reward for his arrest. Lucky for him!
- **I should have seen, someone like Solomon would be lucky**
  - You have to be lucky, to do what he does and still be alive
  - But! He's back on the train and under my control
  - Solomon's luck has run out
  - **My luck holds**

Joe Salvatorre asks true American Patriots to join the movement to SAVE AMERICA

Your support enables us to compete with the liberal globalist money machine and fight for loyal hard-working Americans like you.

Please contribute ANY AMOUNT IMMEDIATELY to keep another election from being stolen from us!

| $250 | $500 | $1,000 | Other |

☑ **Become a member of Joe Salvatorre's True-Blooded America Club, and let Joe know he has your support. Join the cash blitz NOW! We need every Patriot like YOU to stand up so Joe can keep fighting and seize VICTORY in November. Joe will restore Law and Order and help return our country to GREATNESS.**

Make this a weekly recurring donation, and give an additional $250 automatically

Campaign finance law requires us to collect your employment information.
☐ I'm retired.   Employer: _____   Occupation: _____

42

Mack observes law enforcement in action

It feels like forever—though it was probably only minutes—before two unmarked black cars pull up and park in a field by where our train has stopped. Three officers emerge from the cars in a creepily unhurried manner: a tall white balding man with an angular nose like an eagle, a shorter man with red-brown skin and a buzzcut, and a white woman whose blonde hair is pulled tightly back so she looks like a sturdier, tougher version of Reese Witherspoon. Each wears CBP initials across the chests of their matching blue police shirts, their blue pants perfectly creased, a handgun by their right hand and baton by their left.

They're all squinting, even after they enter the observation car.

Two of the CBP officers—Reese and the short guy—are wearing blue ballistic vests over their shirts, with breast pockets full of pens. I guess the pens are there to comfort us, like they're here only to do paperwork. Reese's vest displays a six-digit number; short guy has affixed a Velcro strip to hide his number. They stand to one side of the bar, blocking the passageway to the dining car. The rest of us—there must be a hundred of my fellow passengers crowded in the observation car at this point, shoulder to shoulder and hip to ass—back up a bit to give them space to operate. But we keep open a narrow path down the center of the observation car to where Jimmy Shoulders lies.

"Attention please passengers," says the taller officer. "We are agents of the United States Customs and Border Patrol, here on a routine inspection. We ask that you all have your identification ready to show us. If you are carrying passports for your entry into Canada, we ask to see them too. For those of you who are not citizens of the United States, we ask to see your identifying papers and be prepared to answer our questions about your immigration status."

"You have no right to do this," says a voice somewhere close to the bar. It's Allison. The crowd parts a bit, and I can see her, standing there small, yet solid.

The Representative rushes forward, standing between the officers and Allison, and while his movements are quick, his manner is cool. "Allison," he intones. "These officers have the legal authority to be here, within a reasonable distance from a national boundary."

"There's no way we're within 100 miles of—" begins Allison, but now she's interrupted by the sound of police car sirens blaring. It sounds like a dozen cars, but it turns out to be only three. They race through the same field where CBP has parked, the beacons on their roofs flashing red and blue. They turn sharply in front of the CBP cars. Two officers exit quickly with guns drawn and they enter the train. "Freeze!" says one of them in an icy voice, his gun pointed to the floor.

I freeze.

"The body is back there," the Representative tells them quietly, gesturing towards the balcony of the observation car. One of the police officers, a coffee-skinned woman with freckles I'm sure I'd find gorgeous under different circumstances, moves through the aisle the Representative cleared earlier. When the short CPB officer starts to follow her, he's stopped by the command of the icy-voiced cop.

"Not you."

The tall beaked CBP officer startles so hard, he practically jumps. "We are here on official business," he protests. "We have jurisdiction under U.S. law."

Just then I notice another man emerging from one of the police cars. He is talking on a cell phone, loping towards our train with long, easy steps. His skin is black, darkly so, more African than African American. The other police officers see him, too. And wait.

As the Black cop enters the observation car, I can see the color of his suit, a greyish blue with a bit of iridescence. The man in charge, with a suit like that. He steps to the side of the icy-voiced cop, still holding his cell phone to one ear, and when the beak-nosed CBP officer tries to say something, the cop in the suit holds out his free hand to stop him.

"Please," says the cop in the suit, with pained politeness. "I'm on a call."

Allison appears by my side and takes my arm. The cop in the suit nods to his cell phone and puts it away, inside a suit pocket, just as the freckled cop returns from the back of the car.

"You've found the body, examined it?" asks the cop in the iridescent suit. The freckled cop nods. "Any reason to call the EMTs?" asks the cop in the suit. The freckled cop's eyes widen a little, and her jaw clenches. She shakes her head.

The cop in the suit nods, pauses, then turns back to the beak-nosed CBP officer.

"My name is Robinson Alexander Hamilton," pronounces the CBP officer, in a tone meant to leave an impression, if not a mark. "And we are here on—"

"Jean-Louis LeClerc," replies the cop in the iridescent suit, with an outstretched hand. He has just a hint of an accent. He just barely pronounces the "s" in "Louis." "Washington County Sheriff's Homicide."

"We are here on official business," repeats Alexander Hamilton.

"And you have our complete cooperation," assures LeClerc, "to the fullest extent required by law. If there's someone on this train who spent more than they should at the duty-free store, I promise you, they will face … consequences. But a murder has taken place. For the moment, I'll have to ask you to wait your turn."

"You want us to do what?" Alexander Hamilton is incredulous.

"Thanks for your understanding," LeClerc replies. He then turns back to the freckled cop. "You have identified the victim?" he asks.

"Yes sir," she replies. "His identification is in the wallet in his front left pocket. His name is James Jackson 'Jimmy' Shoulders, a resident of Highland Park, Texas, age 54 years. Occupation, Cowboy Country Singer and Evangelist. Winner of two Grammy Awards."

"How do you know about the Grammy awards?"

"Sir, I guess he somehow persuaded the State of Texas to laminate a reference to those awards on his driver's license."

"I see."

The freckled cop opens a small notebook and consults her notes. "According to a witness in the back of the train, Mr. Shoulders was performing one of his songs from the balcony of the train car when he was shot by an unknown assailant."

LeClerc raises his eyebrows. "Why would he perform from the balcony?"

"So he could be heard, inside and outside the train. Also, he thought the light was better there."

This is when the snobby elderly man with the large gold pen and multiple martinis chooses to speak up from his position on one of the sofas. "You there, Mr. LeClerc," he begins.

"Captain."

Allison grips my arm. But she remains silent.

"Yes, of course—Captain LeClerc," says Snobby Martinis. "But I saw it all. We all did. The murderer of Mr. Shoulders is right there. That Chinese girl." And Snobby Martinis points with his signet ring-clad pinky finger down the train car at May-Bel.

LeClerc opens his mouth, making a little smacking noise. "HER?"

"Yes Captain," says Snobby Martinis. "She shot Mr. Shoulders, with Shoulders' own gun. Probably on orders from the Chinese government."

"And where is that gun now?"

The Representative steps forward. "I have the gun, Captain. The young lady gave it to me. It's in the right outside pocket of my suit jacket." The Representative turns to one side, holding his arms above his head, and Captain LeClerc removes the gun from the Representative's pocket, using a handkerchief so as not to leave fingerprints.

"May-Bel didn't shoot Jimmy Shoulders," shouts one of the accountants from the back of the car. He pushes his way into the aisle between LeClerc and where Shoulders lies. "We were watching, me and my mate. She never raised the gun above her waist. And anyway, she had a camera set up to record Shoulders singing, she wasn't going to intentionally film herself murdering someone!"

"She's a terrorist!" Snobby Martinis snaps back. "She'll post that video on the dark web and become a hero to millions of Chinese and their Maoist sympathizers."

"I don't recall opening the floor for general discussion," LeClerc replies. Then he turns to the freckled cop. "You've already collected the camera? For evidence?" She nods yes in reply.

"Captain LeClerc?" asks the Representative. "Sorry to interrupt the investigation, but I think you should know, the gun you collected from me, it did not kill Mr. Shoulders."

"It didn't."

"No, Captain. It hasn't recently been fired."

"And you can determine this because?"

"Well, I did serve in Afghanistan," says the Representative. "So, I actually know a lot about—"

"Thank you for your service," says Captain LeClerc as he points the gun downward, pops the cylinder out and empties it of cartridges. "I was not in Afghanistan," he continues. "But I concur. I count six bullets and no spent cartridges. These are dummy cartridges as well. Not real bullets."

"That doesn't prove anything," says Snobby Martinis. "Those Chinese are damned clever. She could have substituted fake bullets for the real ones."

"Captain," says the Representative. "If your deputy has examined the body, I think she could add something here about the exit wound."

"I can, sir," confirms the freckled cop. "The bullet appears to have entered the victim's skull through his right cheekbone. The exit wound is ... well, it's a hole of some size ... on the opposite side," she concludes.

"Not a wound made by a six-shooter," LeClerc tells Snobby Martinis. "More likely a high-powered rifle like an AR-15." Snobby Martinis purses his lips.

"So it appears," LeClerc says to the train at large, "Mr. Shoulders was shot by persons unknown, most likely by someone outside of the train, for reasons unknown." He turns to Alexander Hamilton. "Officer Hamilton?"

"Agent," replies Hamilton.

"Agent Hamilton. Feel free to question persons of interest on the train. But under no circumstances may you remove anyone from this train without my permission. If you find anything amiss we will consult, you and I, to determine which of us has the proper jurisdiction to proceed further."

This is when Allison explodes.

"Listen everyone—you have the right to remain silent!" she exclaims to the entire observation car. "Tell Customs and Border Patrol you'll only answer questions in the presence of an attorney. You do not have to answer questions about your immigration status, unless you're here on a visa, and even then you can say you do not want to answer those questions. If they ask to search your belongings, you can say no!"

Above her head, Allison brandishes a small red object for emphasis. It's that little mallet hammer she used to break the glass in her failed attempt in the dining car to stop the train. It's about large enough to check Hamilton's reflexes. Hamilton strides towards Allison, left hand on the baton in his belt, and I move forward to intercept him. "Don't mess with my girlfriend," I tell him. "Or else you'll have to use that baton on me."

I don't know what possessed me to say that.

Luckily, Captain LeClerc lets out an explosive laugh, and pushes both me and Hamilton out of the way. "How do you know all that legal language?" LeClerc questions Allison. Still laughing.

"ACLU protest training," she replies. I expect a confrontation. But instead ... LeClerc SALUTES Allison. Like a fucking French Foreign Legion salute.

"You'd make a good cop," he tells her. Then still smiling he turns to Alexander Hamilton and slaps him on the back, like he had just swallowed a marble. "Hamilton," he says. "You've just been read your Miranda rights."

"Can we begin our questioning now?" asks Hamilton. Not smiling.

"You start from the back of the car," replies LeClerc. "We'll start from the front. And, Agent Hamilton? Try your best to stay out of our way."

"You had better stay out of OUR way."

"Great idea—let's escalate. You can call in the FBI if you like," LeClerc's patience seems to be never ending. "And I can call in state troopers. The Chief Judge of the Northern District of New York is a friend of mine. We could be here for days."

LeClerc is still smiling. He's holding aces.

43

May-Bel has an obstructed view of official proceedings

I am standing towards the back of the Observation Car. I cannot see much. Many Americans are taller than me, and most are also wider than me. People are speaking too quickly for me to use my phone to translate.

I think someone says I shot Jimmy Shoulders. I think someone says I didn't. I think Allison is speaking very loudly about rights.

Here come Allison and Mack to join me. I hug Allison, and she hugs me back, very strongly and for longer than I'm used to. I don't mind.

"Friends," I tell them. I'm not sure they hear. I hope they know.

I tug on Mack's sleeve and pull his ear down to the level of my mouth. "Are you in trouble?" I whisper to him. He stands back up. He nods. He keeps his eyes on what is happening in the center of the car.

44

Diamond decides

"Did you hear what the Black cop said?" Russell hisses in my ear. "We could be here for days. We can't afford that kind of delay."

Russell has moved us subtly towards the front of the observation car, opposite the bar, where there must be three dozen kilted bagpipers perfectly positioned for when the bar reopens. If the bar reopens. I do a quick count. There are more BIPOC law enforcement officers on this train than BIPOC passengers. The only other BIPOC passengers I see—other than the kitchen staff—are the Chinese vlogger and the bagpiper friend of the goth girl, Allison.

Suddenly, I relax. I don't know why. Something about the way Russell is agitated is ... liberating.

"You're the one who wanted to take the train," I tell him. I lean against the arm of the sofa where we sat with our drinks at the train's departure. I look good like that.

But Russell is not paying attention. "Follow my lead," he tells me. "We're getting off this train." And before I can ask him how he's going to manage that, he steps forward. Into the aisle of the observation car, along with Captain LeClerc and Agent Hamilton.

"Excuse me, Agent, there's something you should know," Russell tells Hamilton, in a voice loud enough for everyone to hear. "Mr. Representative, would you hand me that newspaper?" The Representative hands Russell a tabloid-style paper, and Russell unfolds it. And there's the headline, GABRIEL SOLOMON SOUGHT FOR IMMIGRATION CRIMES. "This man, Gabriel Solomon ... is *on this train*. I've previously informed the Representative of this fact, and he told me that Solomon is a fugitive from justice. I've waited to come forward until now, until the authorities boarded the train."

"You're the one who called our office?" Hamilton asks Russell.

"No, that was me," says the Representative.

"What the fuck?" says Allison.

"You again. Your name would be?" LeClerc asks the Representative, with a sigh.

"I am Representative Joe Salvatorre."

"Representing what, exactly?"

"This district. In Congress."

LeClerc tries the Representative's name, twice, aloud. "I know who represents this district. But I remember voting for you, Mr. Salvatorre. Once."

"You've seen Solomon on this train?" snaps Hamilton.

"Um, no," replies the Representative.

"I've seen him," interjects Russell. "Twice."

"You said you never saw him!" Allison shouts.

Russell ignores her as though she were a troublesome undergrad who didn't like the date he chose for the final exam. "One time on the platform," he continues, "before the train got underway." He pauses, looks briefly at me. "Then a second time in the dining car, with that girl." He points at Allison.

"You're a complete liar!" Allison exclaims again. "The Rep AND Mack were there when you told all of us you never saw Gabriel!"

"She saw him too," Russell says, gesturing to me. I feel my eyes widen, I step back, my hands extended outward. No, Russell. Not me.

"And them," Russell says, pointing back at Allison, her friend with the kilt and May-Bel. "They're all trying to help him escape."

Allison is furious. She looks like she'd encircle Russell with both her arms and crush him if she could. But Russell has turned for another quick conversation with the Representative, who in turn speaks inaudibly to Agent Hamilton.

"You can go," Hamilton tells Russell. Who takes a step to leave, only to find his path blocked by LeClerc. Below waist level, his waist, mine, Russell extends a hand to me. Beckoning. His fingers are long and elegant. I've always been a sucker for a man with nice hands. There's his wedding ring, on the fourth finger.

I look at him. He looks back.

His hand drops limp.

LeClerc gestures to a fellow officer, a Black woman, who pats Russell down. Nothing. "Get his address," LeClerc tells the officer. "He's not a subject in my investigation."

"The Representative promised me a police escort out of here," says Russell to LeClerc.

"Hail a cab," is LeClerc's reply. "Or summon an Uber."

45

Mack makes a tactical move

The college professor with the beautiful Black woman—who *was* with the beautiful Black woman—strides out of the train and trudges across the field where the cops and border patrol are parked. It looks like a long walk to a highway, and a longer one to a taxi stand. Does Uber even stop on the highway?

"We'll interview them first," Hamilton says to LeClerc, gesturing towards us—me, Allison and May-Bel. LeClerc nods, resignedly.

"Let me try," the Representative tells Hamilton. The Representative crosses the car and pauses before Allison.

Allison glares back at him, her face turning slightly blue. "You turned out to be something of a Kapo, didn't you Joe?" Allison asks. The Rep looks blank; he doesn't get it. But I do. The word "Kapo" comes up in a lot of Holocaust movies—from *The Sorrow and the Pity* to *Schindler's List*. It's the word Jews used in concentration camps, to describe other Jews who cooperated with and worked for the Nazis.

The Rep turns to me.

"Whatever your young friend may think of me, while I never had any intention of helping Gabriel, I may be inclined to help *you*." He speaks to me while excluding Allison from his line of vision. It's amazing how he can make people disappear from view—another political trick.

"You expect us to continue to trust you," I say with amazement. And he nods.

"Think about it. Why should I help Gabriel? He doesn't stand a chance. We both know he's on this train, and Hamilton's men are going to find him." As if on cue, two more CBP officers enter the observation car, with German Shepherds straining against their leashes. They turn in the other direction, towards the dining car. Hunting prey. Or maybe they're just hungry.

"So," I say. "Is this the 'all politicians are despicable, but I'm better than most' speech?"

"Ha ha," replies the Rep. "You think you're a smart guy, don't you? Then you must know that some of us are here to take advantage of you, and the rest are out to destroy you. I'm firmly in the first camp, and in this world that makes me your best choice."

The Representative lowers his voice. Oh brother. He's going to bargain with me. "I appeal to your warped sense of Latinx Highlander gallantry," he tells me. "Save the girl." He nods his head towards Allison. "Tell us where Solomon is, and I promise she'll face no consequences for trying to protect him."

The Representative makes a kind of sense.

"Go to hell," I tell him anyway. *A somewhat prosaic response*, critiques Inner Mack. *On the other hand, I'm sure that in a week you will come up with something better when you tell your mother and sister about this ... presuming you're not in jail.*

Prosaic or not, my response does the job with the Representative. He shrugs and turns away. "Your move, Agent Hamilton," he says.

Hamilton strides to Allison. "I suggest you forget about the ACLU," he tells her. "You're in a lot of trouble. The best thing you can do is cooperate with us. You understand?"

"Yes," she answers.

"Good!" Hamilton says, opening up a little notebook and writing with a pencil he might have found at a miniature golf course. "Your name, last name first."

Allison remains silent. It seems strangely unnatural, coming from her.

"Young lady," Hamilton warns Allison. "Whatever you think your rights are, you have to answer my questions."

"Allison Muth," says the Representative from behind Hamilton. Hamilton writes this down.

"Address?" asks Hamilton.

"320 Sycamore, Bedford Hills, New York," answers Allison. I bite my lip, because this is Jimmy Stewart and Donna Reed's address in *It's A Wonderful Life*. Are we the only people on this train who watch movies?

You know, I'm a little like Jimmy Stewart, tall and adorably gawky. I can't quite imagine Allison as Donna Reed, but what I'm experiencing is clearly some kind of postmodern mashup picture, and Allison is Madonna from *Desperately Seeking Susan*.

"Reason for this trip?" asks Hamilton.

"It's the slowest way I know to get home," Allison replies, and when Hamilton looks up to protest, she adds, "Really. I told the truth that time."

"Now, Ms. Muth. Tell us what you know about Gabriel Solomon."

"Tell me what you know about putting Brown babies in cages."

Hamilton's neck snaps back a bit. "I don't have to tell you—"

"Tell me what you know about refugees imprisoned by Customs and Border Patrol in *hieleras*, iceboxes, small concrete hellholes, no beds, no sanitation, sleeping on concrete floors for weeks at a time, right here in America."

"Young lady, I don't work at the southwest—"

"Hypocrite, murderer, Nazi." Each word hangs in the air like a caption.

"Ignore her," says Tirtov, from seemingly out of nowhere. I hadn't noticed him in the crowd before. He has lost his Beatles wig, and now looks like a deranged Yul Brynner on a coffee break from *Westworld*. He makes a dismissive gesture in Allison's direction.

Hamilton protests. "Sir, she's a—"

"She is Jew," Tirtov says. "A *zhydivka*. Born to lie, and whore." And he spits. On the carpet of the fancy old-time train. "Just ask him. The man in the skirt."

I try a cleansing breath. It is no more than a rasp. *Stay focused*, warns Inner Mack.

Hamilton's face feels like it's about three inches from mine. "Name?" he snarls at me.

I try to place myself in a movie, detective Philip Marlowe on a wooden chair in police headquarters, hands cuffed behind me, standing up to the interrogation of a hard veteran cop with a blackjack in one hand and brass knuckles on the other.

"I don't have to tell you shit," is the reply that emerges from my lips. Not so much Philip Marlowe as Shaggy from Scooby-Doo. But it's all I've got.

That's when something occurs to me. I've got Gabriel's wallet in my sporran! Where I put it after he changed into my kilt at the Moretz station. *Play this cool*, advises Inner Mack, with some urgency.

"You don't have to be nice to him," Tirtov says, moving forward. "Look at him. Salvadoran. I heard him say so. He has no rights here."

"Show me your identification, and any immigration papers you are carrying," Hamilton tells me.

I don't move.

And this is when Tirtov reaches for his handgun. I don't know jack about guns. But this isn't a rootin' tootin' six-shooter like Jimmy Shoulders'. Tirtov's is dull black, no cylinder, no hammer, and its trigger guard is almost square shaped. I would not want to twirl one of these around my finger.

"Put it away, Tirtov." That's LeClerc's voice. Moving in my direction.

"I have a Second Amendment right to carry—"

"Not in New York State, you don't."

"I am a sovereign citizen," Tirtov mutters. But he pulls his pants up even higher, so they ride at about ribcage level, and sticks his weapon inside his waistband.

"Let's get you out of here in one piece, son," LeClerc tells me, sounding a little more cowboy and a little less Caribbean. "Start by telling them your name."

I hesitate. May-Bel murmurs, "Create a distraction, kilt-boy, I have an idea." Or was she just thinking that? Like I said, I hear people's thoughts sometimes.

The second wallet, Inner Mack reminds me. *In your sporran.*

Damn. There are a lot of voices.

"My name is Gabriel Solomon," I say.

"That isn't Gabriel!" shouts a voice. The Representative's this time. "Gabriel is an older man. Wearing a plaid scarf."

I reach into my sporran, for Gabriel's wallet. I don't rush it. Inside my sporran, I find first ... something soft and cozy to the touch. I had forgotten this was there. I remove Gabriel's scarf from the sporran and put it on. Slowly. I hear Allison to one side of me take in a slow breath.

Time slows. This is like the best moments of being a teacher. You're about to say something important, and the students know it. They fix their eyes on you, waiting. I look out through the train windows. It has become quite dark outside. I reach back into the sporran for Gabriel's wallet, and remove the driver's license I find there. I read it, then hand it to Hamilton and improvise a bit. "I am Salvadorian. A citizen of Canada. Here is my driver's license from the Province of Ontario, perfectly valid."

From behind Hamilton, Tirtov snorts.

"His name is Mack," says the Representative. "Mack ... something."

It helps sometimes to have a name too long for most people to remember.

"I have a photo of Gabriel!" exclaims the Representative. "It's in today's newspaper. Where is that paper?"

I know where the paper is. It's with that professor guy. Probably in Uber comfort by now.

Oh my fucking God. This plan could actually work.

That's when I feel the blow to my face, from a leather glove. Tirtov's. He's slapped me with the open end of the glove, and there's a button on the end, small and sharp. I taste blood. I lunge for him, and directly into a straight arm from Hamilton. Who has played this part before. Deftly he spins me by one shoulder so my back is to him, then wraps one arm around my neck. Choking.

"I HAVE SOMETHING TO SAY," announces May-Bel from somewhere a foot below me, in a voice I wouldn't have guessed she possesses. Sharp. Loud.

"My name is Zhang Mei. I am a citizen of the People's Republic of China. I am here in the United States without papers, without permission. I am here to claim asylum and demand to be taken to the nearest clinic to exercise my right, my freedom, to terminate my pregnancy."

She places one hand over her belly to tell us, this is hers, not ours.

"Seize her!" screams Tirtov. The observation car breaks into pandemonium.

"What about Gabriel?" asks Hamilton. Who has tossed me aside like I'm unwanted trash.

"THE HELL WITH GABRIEL!" Tirtov is in a panic. "SAVE THE UNBORN CHILD!"

At this moment, the observation car plunges into darkness.

46

Tiffany Tolliver calls it a wrap

Don't panic, Representative. Not here in your campaign headquarters, in front of all your staff. No matter what you're paying them. Act more like Tirtov. He's no more volatile than usual.

No, Vladimir, don't take this as a sign to act MORE dramatic. You've done quite enough scenery chewing during this production.

We'll make the storyline work.

That drama ... the cops fighting with Homeland Security, the Chinese girl pleading for asylum ... that's great content. And Jimmy Shoulders got a big feature and the President's base can't get enough of him.

Yes, Jimmy Shoulders is dead. He's a martyr now. Or, a traitor to everything he said he believed in. I'm not sure which. We'll see which plays better in post-production.

What's in it for you, Tirtov? Plenty. You want to please your friends in the Russian mafia? A word from the President will do it. You can add the Chinese now to your little list of internal enemies. And your northeast border version of the posses on the southwest border ... well, that posse is on the map now.

What's in it for you, Representative? Plenty. You want your own reality show? Doable—I'll put in a good word. After all, this whole adventure was thanks to some intel I got from someone inside the Department of Health. That's how I got YOUR name.

What's in it for me, Ms. Tiffany Tolliver, wannabe look-alike to the real President's real daughter? A big job, and an even bigger ... relationship.

You want to know why I picked this storyline? Where better to look for material than at classic movies? As an old man, Hitchcock remade some of his earlier films, bringing them up to date. He'd like my mashup, or should I say, remake. That's my auteur theory.

So use the moment, Representative. Look at me admiringly with a slight smile playing on your lips as you consider how my prestige has been enhanced by this adventure. This mission makes it clear I'm a winner. Look at all I've created! Imagine where it will appear. TikTok. Fox News. Eventually the Library of Congress. I know how to control people and I know all the right people to control. Even better, I know where to place the cameras. All over the train.

And you, Tirtov, will look good too. It's like what you say about Americans and conspiracy theories. It's easy to draw them into one. Everyone wants to be in the movies.

That's it, both of you. Keep gazing at me respectfully, with just a patina of sexual longing. What the cameras miss, we'll add with CGI.

Vape.

True, Gabriel got away. I was not expecting that. But the upside is, I saved the cost to either dispose of his dead body or pay him off. And by doing so, I brought this project in under budget. We will still make the President money. Nothing has changed for the worse.

I'll add some private footage later. Just for the President. I think—I hope—he'll like it.

I'm not the daughter he had. I'm the daughter he wishes he'd had. The one he deserves.

And ... cut.

47

May-Bel makes more American friends

Greetings, travel fans! This is May-Bel the happy train vlogger. Only as you can see, I am not on a train. I am the guest of the United States government, travelling in a government car to Canada to join my fellow Chongqing University students to fly back to China.

Wow! What a crazy end to my journey on the Voyages Rétro special train. As you know from my vlog, somebody shot poor Mr. Jimmy Shoulders. What you did not see was when the police came to solve the mystery of who shot Mr. Shoulders ... and like in any good mystery, the police named many suspects. Even I was a suspect!

So here is an important travel tip. If you find yourself in a bad situation with the police in a foreign country, follow the advice of my good friend Allison and REMAIN SILENT. Especially in America, you have the right to remain silent. This is a good right, much better than the freedom to own so many guns! I think the spirit of Jimmy Shoulders would agree with that.

But May-Bel your happy train vlogger made a mistake and did not remain silent. And, my ability to speak English isn't so good when I'm excited and try to speak quickly. So, the police did not understand when I tried to say that I am in the United States on a student trip. They thought I said that I was in the United States illegally! And ... so crazy ... they also thought I said I was pregnant!

In the United States, they care very much if you're pregnant. So right after I forgot to remain silent, the police took me immediately to a medical facility to make sure I am all right. This is very prompt medical care! Of course they discovered I am not pregnant, and also that I have a good travel visa and am part of a group of Chinese university students making friends in America. The police were embarrassed they made a mistake, and they said they were sorry for taking me off the special train. I said I was even more sorry for my English being so poor and not saying things clearly. Problem solved!

Except, the problem was not solved. I was supposed to meet my student travel group in Merveilleux City to fly home to China, and I was late! The special train was gone, and I did not know how to travel by myself to Merveilleux City. Also, the police in the United States were saying to me, could you please stay here with us a little longer? I did not want to stay, but I also wanted to be polite and cooperate with the police. I was able to speak to the Director of our student travel group, and she was very upset with me for delaying everyone after they had given me special permission to travel on the Voyages Rétro train. I was being irresponsible! So I was worried because I was delaying all my fellow students, and maybe some of them have a spouse at home waiting for them, like I do. This is terrible!

But then I got a second phone call from the Director, and it was a totally different phone call. She said, everyone is proud of me, and of course I should stay in the United States and cooperate with the police.

I was very confused—why was she happy now, and why was everyone proud of me? The Director explained, "Because you are helping the police fight political corruption, and corruption is a terrible thing everywhere." These two different phone calls were surprising. I had to sit down with my eyes closed and take deep breaths. I even did a little Tai Chi. Thank you to my friend Allison for reminding me how helpful Tai Chi can be!

Then I asked someone at the police station, could I please talk to someone about the political corruption? So they took me to a special room with a big table, and there were many police people there, and they had my vlogging camera and my two microphones. They said they were looking at my camera and listening to my microphones for clues about who shot Jimmy Shoulders, when they came across my conversation with Congressman Joe! And I said, I was so sorry, he did ask me to keep the conversation off the record, but I must have made a mistake and turned the microphone on instead of off. But they said no, no, I did not do anything wrong, and that they suspected Congressman Joe was asking people who do not live in the United States to give him money for his election. My microphone, they said, contains evidence that Congressman Joe asked me and my father for money. This is a corrupt practice! This is against the law!

So of course I said they could keep the microphone, and they thanked me very much. They also asked if I would come back to the United States and talk to a grand jury about how I recorded my talk with Congressman Joe, and how the talk made me feel. I answered that my government in China would have to say ok, and they told me my government has already said ok. Wow!

The police said I should go home to China for a while, and then they would fly me to New York to talk to the grand jury. I said, maybe they could fly me to San Francisco instead, or Los Angeles? So I can take the train to New York. For my vlog!

I wonder. If I am allowed to travel by train from Los Angeles to New York ... would Allison and Mack travel with me? That would be fun!

Also I think those two are never going to be romantic together unless I help.

Signing off, it's May-Bel, the happy train vlogger, even more happy than usual. Until next time!

48

Mack gets there

"Where should I drop you?" Allison says to me as we ride down the streets of Merveilleux City in a taxi that she—once again—is paying for.

"I'll just get off when you do," I say. Then I fall silent. I'm thinking about what happened when the lights went out on the train, and how lucky we are to be heading over to ... well, I'm not sure where we're heading over to.

When the lights went out, LeClerc pulled me into the kitchen and scared the hell out of me to such an extent that I produced my actual ID and explained that I got punched in the face by the now defunct cowboy and didn't quite know what I was doing. I added something about being very close to getting my teaching credential. "And anyway," I vaguely remember managing to stammer, "isn't what Gabriel Solomon doing kind of a good thing?" LeClerc responded by shaking his head at me in wonder. "You're lucky you're not lying back there with Jimmy Shoulders," he told me. Then he put his fingers over his lips, collected Gabriel's wallet from me, walked back to the observation car and announced that in the darkness Gabriel Solomon had escaped the train (which, technically seems to be true ... I wonder if he ever found his pants?). LeClerc and the rest of his law enforcement gang got off the train carrying the corpse of Jimmy Shoulders. The train proceeded on its way and we were permitted entry into Canada.

We arrived at the station at Merveilleux City CENTRE VILLE, with our luggage and my pipes all intact. I stepped off the train just in time to see the Shoulders kid AND his mom being greeted by a couple in t-shirts reading: "NO PERSON IS ILLEGAL/PERSON-NE N'EST ILLÉGAL."

Now I sit in the taxi wondering how we all managed to evade arrest. All except for May-Bel. Hamilton and Homeland Security carted her off the train for ... actually, I don't know exactly what for. I do know she saved the day, with that distraction about needing an abortion. That was a brilliant performance on her part.

Your own performance wasn't bad either, says Inner Mack. Which throws me for a loop. I don't know how to cope with an admiring inner voice.

"We have to go to the Chinese Consulate," I tell Allison. "I'm not sure what good it will do but we have to try to help May-Bel."

Allison is quiet, because she is looking at her phone and smiling.

"Look," she says.

"Greetings, travel fans, this is May-Bel the happy train vlogger," says the voice from Allison's phone. "Only as you can see, I am not on a train."

"She's ok!" we both say at the same time.

Then we get quiet again.

I guess this means I can still participate on my panel, "Pipe Bands in Southern California," and enjoy the rest of the conference I've travelled all the way across the country to attend. I guess I'd feel happy if I weren't thinking about something else.

Namely, I'm wondering how to say something I don't even have the words for—that I ... not just like ... but ... maybe love Allison. How do you even say all that to someone you've only known a few hours without sounding like an idiot? In a cab, yet?

While I'm thinking, we pull up in front of a fancy hotel. It's an old-style grand building with flowers everywhere. In pots and in baskets. Here, it feels like spring has arrived after all. There's a big sign out front:

Hotel Holbein, Merveilleux

"There's a conference here I need to go to," she says. "The World Religions Studies Conference."

I squint. This is all news to me—her attending a conference.

We walk into the lobby. At the bar by the entrance, I see a large group circling someone speaking rhythmic words in powerful, resonant tones. I know that voice. I catch a glimpse of long braids waving as the head that owns them moves dramatically.

"Epic!" somebody shouts. Applause. The clinking of glasses.

We walk past registration and see people in business attire darting around the elevators with those dumb nametags that people always wear at conventions. But we also notice young people with dyed pink and blue hair, braids and fades and buzz cuts, man buns and ponytails, torn jeans, flowing skirts and cowboy boots. All shouldering tote bags that say *American Writers and Publishers Association*.

Scattered among the suits and book people are nuns in habits, ministers with their weird collars, and monks in robes with crucifixes hanging off them. And darting around *them* are—of course—pipers in their various tartans.

"What are there—like ten conventions going on here at the same time?" I say to Allison.

"Who cares?" she says. "Let's go in here."

We walk into a ballroom that's empty except for some scattered chairs and a table at the front of the room with a design on it. Guys in red robes are doing something to the design, and on the occasional chair, others sit and watch.

"They're making a sand mandala," Allison says.

"Sand?" I say.

"Meant to be impermanent," she says. "They'll finish it, and then they'll disperse it."

Well, says Inner Mack, *at least you're not at the beach.*

In the corners of this big room are small groups of people, like not more than five or six standing in little huddles. We walk over to one of them. Two people dressed in black are demonstrating these big dolls and moving them around.

"They help folks understand stories," one enthusiastic extremely tall girl says to the others. "But the story you tell is up to you."

I'm hearing a lot of thoughts. Well, not thoughts exactly. Colors of thoughts, all rapidly moving fluidly from person to person.

"They're not dolls," Allison explains. "They're Bunraku puppets, used in the Danker puppet plays I told you about."

"Why are we here?" I ask, as people in the circle take turns holding the puppets. One of a lady, and one of a monkey. And one of an octopus.

"I need to give them a message from Henry Holbein ... he can't travel just now."

"Holbein ... that's the hotel chain we're in, right?"

Allison takes an envelope out of her pocket. It's got an octopus seal on it.

"What does the message say?"

"Listen," she says, and then she just looks at me. I look back into those deep green eyes. I hear her:

The message says: **Don't Give Up. Keep on performing. Change the play any way you want. It doesn't even have to have puppets. Tell the stories that matter to you and your community.**

And here's the account # for the funds you need to keep the learning circles going.

The tall girl interrupts our thought exchange.

"In a sense, whenever we perform physically, we are puppeteers. Manipulating our outer selves. To express something deeper."

"Like what professional wrestlers do," I say.

"Well, get you and your deepiosity," Allison says, smiling. She lifts her chin very slightly and the tall girl looks her way. Allison hands the envelope to her, and she calmly puts it in her pocket.

"So—who's the octopus?" I ask, pointing at the puppet.

"That depends," the tall girl says. "It might be *Akkorokamui*, Shinto deity of benevolence and healing, or it might be the Great Goddess, whose powers were distorted into the Gorgon of Greek Mythology. It's also a symbol used by Climate Strike and the Women's March."

I pull Allison aside to where the monks are slowly pouring sand onto the table.

"So, you're an activist too?" I say.

"I'm really just a messenger," she says. "Like I told Gabriel."

"What are you doing, when you aren't delivering secret messages to a Canadian hotel?"

"I'm a college dropout." I nod. That part, at least, sounds right.

"I just happen to be in between no-future careers, and I'm trying to do a little bit of good in this fucked-up world. I mean—isn't that what a religion does?"

"So—are you a—what do you call it—Danker?" I ask.

"Let's say I'm a combination Jewish and Danker."

"Is that like a Janker?"

"That sounds incredibly stupid," she says, and starts laughing.

"We're not a cult," another tall girl is explaining to another small group. "We're sharing the space with the Buddhist monks because we are a progressive philosophy rather than a set of doctrines."

"That's what my aunt said about the Moonies," I observe. "Then we had to kidnap her from the Rancho Santa Fe compound to get her out."

That's when Allison starts hitting me.

"I'm kidding!" I cry, as she punches my arm repeatedly. "Are all you Jankers so sensitive?"

"You are so fucking obnoxious!" she says. But she's still laughing, because—let's face it, I'm pretty funny.

We watch the monks in red pour sand onto the design, and then manipulate it with instruments that look like straws. A couple of little girls come into the room. They take two chairs and go and stand on them; they can look down at the monks while they arrange the sand into the picture. It's an incredibly intricate work.

You need a lot of patience to make art.

A gong rings, and the monks begin chanting. Which reminds me.

"I have to go register at the pipe convention," I say, "but I'll be back later, and we'll eat something?"

"Yeah—we never got to eat!" Allison says. "I'll be here unless I go out for a cigarette."

"I'll be back in 20 minutes tops," I say. "Just please don't do any acid. And ... you should quit smoking."

"Don't lose your bagpipes," she says, "and stop whitening your teeth. You look like an android."

She's about to say something else insulting, but she can't because I kiss her. It's not a big kiss, it's not a long one, but it *is* one. Her lips are soft. Our lips don't grab, but they do linger. It feels promising.

You should have kissed her earlier, in the cab, complains Inner Mack.

For once I let my better self have the last word. I walk out of the ballroom and into the lobby. I go to the concierge's desk.

"How far is the convention center from here?" I ask her.

"It's just across the bridge," the concierge says, pointing up. "All the hotels here are connected to the convention center—spokes around a wheel."

I look up and see one bridge, but in the distance I feel like I see others crisscrossing the dome of the building. Going on and on in multiple directions.

I thank her and go up the escalator. I'm thinking about how I'm going to prepare some lesson plans on religion. People are always afraid to talk about it. But students should read some of the religious texts of the past—we should talk about those ideas—how we first started thinking about how we can live together.

Inner Mack says, *You can do that. You <u>will</u> do it.*

"JUST ASK ONE OF THE PIPERS FROM THE TRAIN," someone shouts.

Right ahead of me at the top of the escalator is a group of people surrounding two guys wearing shiny underwear, glittery cloaks, and big leather belts encrusted with fake gems. Professional wrestlers! *They're wearing the wrestling gear you saw in the baggage car on the train!* realizes Inner Mack. And he's right. I wonder where these guys were the whole journey.

The two wrestlers flex and yell as people on both sides take pictures and ask for selfies with them. A few feet away, some beleaguered guy mans a table selling t-shirts and mugs with their ring names on them: **Fernando Amor** and **Le Salaud.**

It's a promo.

"We're holding this press conference so our fans know we were late for the show today because we are set upon by villains posing as GOOD PEOPLE," one wrestler proclaims. "But we fought our way out and we'll beat the crap out of anybody who stands between us and victory at **La Défiance – Super-Extrême**! We deserve and demand a challenge to the top of the card!"

The second wrestler pushes the first aside and growls at me over the heads of the crowd. "TELL THEM what happened, HIGH-LANDER! And play us a tune!"

I get off the escalator and grin as the smart phones turn towards me. I stand up straight, so I can inflate the bag of my bagpipe. When I stand up very straight, I'm easy to spot even in a crowd.

See, I get my height from my dad.

49

Letter of complaint regarding a recent journey to the north

Vintage Travel Trains/Voyages rétro en train
   Salazar Évident, CEO board of directors
   190 Avenue Phillipe Quai Dique
   Merveilleux City, Québec, CANADA G1A 1SB

Dear Sir:

I am (or at least, I *have* been) one of your frequent U.S. travelers, and as such, I am writing to complain about the strange and highly disquieting incidents that occurred upon train number 002 traveling from Narrow Interior MA to Merveilleux City on March 10th, 20—-.

I was traveling as is my custom in the first-class compartment, because I enjoy the quiet luxury that your trains *usually* provide. In fact, I was about to continue my writing of a poem in heroic couplets about the Iraq War, when I was interrupted by an extremely shrill and unpleasantly loud female voice.

I left my compartment because it was time for my usual round of martinis, but I was blocked in the hallway from proceeding further. There was an ongoing extremely loud conversation between the shrill female I just mentioned and a Hispanic man clad, incredibly, in a kilt.

The girl was insisting that her companion on the train, a Mr. Something, had vanished without a trace. Poof! Before I could speak, the two of them pushed past me without so much as a how do you do, and began searching for this supposedly missing person, careening through the dining car, the observation car, and (I later learned) the luggage compartment. There, they undoubtedly disturbed my show dogs, who deplore air travel, and who insist on a more grounded form of transport.

I took a seat in the observation car and settled in for some serious lyrical composition. But it became ne'er impossible to continue working on my elegy in progress, given the continual caterwauling of these two about the missing person. I tried to impress upon them that they were behaving in a ridiculous manner, to no effect. Even the attempts of an attractive, clearly successful candidate for congressional office (wearing a Brooks Brothers suit, and, if I'm not mistaken, carrying a Coach briefcase), were of no avail. He could not convince the girl that she was imagining things, and the boy seemed determined to support her.

I returned to my (finally) quiet deluxe compartment and what followed, as they say in French, was *le comble*.

I gazed out the window, collecting my thoughts to compose several crucial lines about Mosul and the struggles of our forces there—how successful they were, how successful they must be for the very fact that they are part of the greatest empire ever created. While you Canadians may not approve of the prior U.S. president, it must be admitted that he and his cabinet manifested a passion for success and power that is sadly lacking in the young people of this country and of which, frankly, we need *much* more.

But suddenly I saw the Female climbing, or should I say swimming, along the side of the train, her arms having been turned into giant tentacles. She suctioned herself right up to my window.

Then she halted.

Her blue face pressed against the glass in a truly horrifying manner. Her eyes bulged an unnatural shade of green, and her black beak opened to reveal jagged teeth and a huge red tongue. The tongue spun out, and indeed it extended out so far and pressed against the window with such force that I thought it would break the very glass that separated us. For a moment I thought that gaping maw would penetrate the barrier and swallow me whole, whereby I would slowly languish in a semi-digested state within her innards. It would be dark inside the octopus girl, and I would hear only her rumbling roar as she tore through the deep, consuming everything in her path.

But I could not turn my eyes away from hers either. The giant green eyes grasped my own terrified oculars, and held.

I fainted.

I came to, staggered back out to the observation car, and replenished myself with several more martinis. What more could I do?

In retrospect, it has occurred to me that I was part of one of these godforsaken reality shows where one uses real people and situations, on a budget, to create unsustainable story lines. But this plot is stupid. What IS an octopus-woman doing on a train going to Canada anyway? There's no ocean here. But I digress.

Furthermore, my arrival in Merveilleux City was severely delayed due to the following:

The train made an unscheduled stop before the border, where we were boarded by not one, but two arms of law enforcement, who,

I might add, were shockingly uninterested in what was *really* going awry on your train. Instead of interrogating a Chinese operative, law enforcement focused on the death of some cowboy entertainer. They also ignored the presence of two professional wrestlers, one of whom was an Arab.

If that wasn't enough, the bartender had the nerve to pour me a martini made entirely of bourbon.

AND then the final insult: my best Brooks Brothers suit-pants were STOLEN from my travel case and replaced with a hideous-looking red kilt.

Please do not insult my intelligence with the usual disclaimer: *Mr. Peabody, we regret the inconvenience, but everything was sorted in the end. You received your luggage shortly after your arrival in Merveilleux City, and you were reimbursed for half your first-class ticket because of the confusion.*

Nothing was sorted. Who shot the cowboy? WHERE ARE MY PANTS? What does the appearance of the kilt in my suitcase portend?

Is the Department of Defense secretly experimenting—again—with the creation of mutants? Are these experiments related to some secret mission to Scotland? Involving the Loch Ness project?

Fair enough, but please NOT on my luxury train ride!

In conclusion, I am writing to complain, not merely about the inconvenience and the terror, **but about the state of mind that your company has placed me in.** I am complaining because, the more I think about it, the more I commence having doubts about *the very fabric of the society we live in.* Is pacifism practical? Should unemployed people perhaps have shelter and food? Mightn't it just be easier to open all our borders? Legalize drugs? Might the universal basic income idea have actual legs?

They are masters of evasion, you know. Octopuses. Marvelously flexible. They can stretch and contract. They can escape any container.

I watch them at the aquarium in Boston. I've been going there every day.

I am sincerely —

Spencer Peabody, Esq. III

333 Beacon Hill

Boston, MA 02108

THE END

Acknowledgments

Journey to Merveilleux City was a tantalizing yet maddeningly difficult story to write. I'm grateful to poet/librettist Neil Aitken who made several crucial suggestions during the course of multiple readings of the manuscript, and to Robert Gross who also read several drafts of this novella and encouraged me about it. Ruthie Marlenée, Mary Anne Perez and liz gonzález gave helpful advice on the opening pages of Mack's adventures, and were endlessly supportive. Thank you! I read an early version of Mr. Peabody's letter to a group of Whidbey Writers Workshop friends. I thank them for their friendship and enthusiasm.

My Whidbey MFA classmate FeLicia Elam related with generosity and honesty what it was like to be a Black writer surrounded by a predominantly white cohort of teachers and students. Nadine Pinede shared her own unique perspective on the Whidbey program as a Haitian-Canadian writer. Both of these friends influenced my development of the character of Diamond Williams. Diamond is a fictional character for sure, yet her brilliance, heroism, and persistence are mirrored in the lives and writing of the Black women writers I have had the honor of encountering, among them: Dana Johnson, Tashi Ko, Tananarive Due, Natashia Deón, Nancy Rawles, and the late Celena Diana Bumpus. Poets Romaine Washington, bridgette bianca, Lynne Thompson, Pam Ward, Morgan Parker, and Camari Carter-Hawkins inspire me with their genius and energy.

Owen Torres has kindly shared with me his experiences in grad school as well as his enduring love for pipe bands. He has also shared his ideas regarding the challenges of teaching K-12. His passion for and commitment to teaching are continually inspiring and profound.

Professional wrestlers are incredible artist-performers who bring together dance, tumbling, martial arts, *comedia del arte,* and pantomime, to create an experience that you need to see live to appreciate. I am grateful to these artists for bringing us vitality, energy, emotionality, physicality, and a sincerity that is unique and special. This entire world was made understandable to me by the social commentator, writer, and podcaster Elby Hunktears and by the writers they fostered and published at fanbyte.com. I am grateful to the Defiance Promotion in Seattle, and to Pro Wrestling Guerilla of Los Angeles, where I first learned to pick up my folding chair and get out of the way of wrestlers hurtling out of the ring.

Thanks to Professor Vivian-Lee Nyitray and her husband Douglas Oliver, I had the honor of visiting the Prospect College campuses in the People's Republic of China as a writer in residence and master teacher in 2015. The character of May-Bel is a composite of the students and faculty I met in Chongqing and Shanxi Province, who were unfailingly gracious, friendly, and compelling. To the person, they had a sense of wit and perspective that my husband and I continue to wonder at.

I am grateful to the remarkable Shannon Phillips at Picture Show Press for her support of this unusual book project, and for Picture Show's support of the novella as a form.

Alfred Hitchcock's films fascinated me as a child, and his movies' ability to surprise, terrify, and delight me continues. Thank you, Mr. Hitchcock, in particular for *The 39 Steps*, *North by Northwest*, and *The Lady Vanishes*.

My mother and maternal grandmother loved trains, and I went on my first train journeys with them when I was four. I travelled Europe with my spouse Larry Behrendt on a Eurail Pass 40 years ago, and in November 2022 he and I rode a train from Richmond, Virginia to New York City—where we met a woman with an incredible story. Thank you Larry for believing in my own strange attempt to tell a train tale, for serving as continuity editor, and for creating the lyrics to "Jesus Is My Kind of Cowboy."

And thank you to all the storytellers I have met and hope to meet on trains.

In doing research for this project, I became aware of the global community devoted to promoting and documenting train travel, including numerous travel vloggers like May-Bel. I am particularly indebted to the unnamed creator of the Solo Solo Travel YouTube channel. Like (I imagine) many of you, I truly wish that there was a train like the one in this novel travelling from the northeast United States into Canada. I also wish for expanded train service within the United States.

If you are curious about the fictional Dankers, you can learn more about them in my novel *The Puppet Turners of Narrow Interior* (Urban Farmhouse Press) and the novelette *Rescue Plan* (Bamboo Dart Press).

I don't know of any organization like the one in the book providing assistance to those whose survival depends on avoiding U.S. immigration authorities. But Larry and I have the privilege to help support organizations in the United States that legally provide refugees and asylum seekers with much-needed assistance. The character of Gabriel Solomon is intended to stand in for the many white allies of these organizations, but should not be understood as representative of their overall leadership. The organizations we support are most often led by members of the immigrant communities impacted by U.S. immigration policy, a policy that is often tragically inhumane, unjust and violative of our national and religious ethos of welcoming the downtrodden and the stranger. You can find incomplete lists of these organizations at stories.avvo.com/rights/immigration/10-nonprofit -organizations-help-immigration.html and nnirr.org/programs/seek ing-border-justice/border-advocacy-groups. And write your elected leaders about immigration reform, and the pathway to citizenship for Dreamers.